Pilgrim's River

By

Wyn Hughes

Pilgrim's River is a work of fiction. Names, characters and incidents are either the product of the author's imagination or are used fictitiously. Any resemblance to actual persons, living or dead, or events is entirely coincidental.

Copyright © 2014
By
Wyn Hughes

All rights reserved

Table of Contents

Pilgrim's River
Table of Contents
Chapter 1
Chapter 2
Chapter 3
Chapter 4
Chapter 5
Chapter 6
Chapter 7
Chapter 8
Chapter 9
Chapter 10
Chapter 11
Chapter 12
Chapter 13
Chapter 14
Chapter 15
Chapter 16
Chapter 17
Chapter 18
Chapter 19
Chapter 20

Chapter 21
Chapter 22
Chapter 23
Chapter 24
Chapter 25
Chapter 26
Chapter 27
Epilogue
About the Author

Chapter 1

The sun kissed the horizon, bringing a perfect English summer's day to a close, and there was nowhere better to witness its crimson glory than on a boat off Devon's south coast. Start Bay shimmered in the setting sun, whose rays began to throw long shadows over the cliffs east of Blackpool sands. Under full sail in a gentle north westerly breeze, I was headed for the mouth of the river Dart where a myriad of small sailboats were enjoying the last of the evening light, undoubtedly preparing for the upcoming Royal Regatta, for which Dartmouth's was famous. Most of the boats were heading back upriver, tacking against an ebbing tide in full flow, and against a northerly element to the wind, testing their sailing skills to the limit.

As the mediaeval Dartmouth and Kingswear castles on either side of the estuary came into view, I decided to fire up the diesel, truth be told to get to the pub quicker. I furled the headsails and mizzen, left the mainsail and settled back in the cockpit looking forward to that first pint of Doom Bar, which would slip down without touching the sides. Without warning, the boat juddered and the engine cut out, but worst of all the wheel stiffened and I lost steerage just as I entered the narrowest part of the marked channel. I guessed that the prop had picked up a discarded fishing net or some other debris carelessly thrown overboard by another boat and peered over the transom where a large dark object ominously appeared below water in the shadows of the increasing gloom. "I don't bloody believe it", I swore, as I realised that my perfect day was about to come to a watery and cold end.

My first priority was to ensure that the now drifting 'Pilgrim', with no helm, floated safely on the outflowing current towards the open sea using nothing but the sails to guide her out of harm's way. Having furled the mainsail, I used the staysail, sometimes backing it to the wind to steer the boat until I was satisfied that we were out of danger from the rocks flanking the mouth of the river. I went below to change into my swim shorts and to retrieve my tool belt into which I put my trusty army issue knife and a gruesome looking hand saw. Complete with mask and snorkel, and having secured a line to the aft cleat, tying it around my waist to ensure the current didn't carry me away from the boat, I lowered myself down the transom ladder and into the cold water of the English Channel.

What greeted me was a bulky sack-like mass that had wrapped itself around the prop and in the process had jammed itself in such a position that the rudder could not move in any direction. I came up for air thankful that there did not appear to be any damage, although it would be a slow process to hack off the offending object in the fading light. What the hell it was I had no idea, but I cursed my luck at having been the unfortunate vessel to have hooked it. Down again and under the hull, I grabbed the prop shaft to hold myself down and for leverage.

With knife in hand I systematically cut the material as close to the prop as I could, eventually cutting an opening from which popped the most gruesome sight I have ever witnessed. Out of the bag sprang a badly decomposed human head, which I assumed was still attached to the rest of its body, and in my panic to return to the surface, I hit my head several times on the hull and finally on the ladder, and in my dazed state, climbed up onto the swim platform and plonked myself down with my feet in the water. What the hell to do next? I certainly had no urge to get back in the water and confront this bloated and decomposing corpse, but knew that before I could return to the dock, some more underwater hacking would be required.

First though, the authorities would have to be informed, so I climbed back on-board and made my way below. I reached for the VHF intending to call the Coastguard on channel 16, but had second thoughts as it would be an open channel which all and sundry would monitor. I found my mobile phone and called Brixham Coastguard hoping my old mate Jack Oliver was on duty. The phone rang twice and was answered "Brixham Coastguard Station, how may we help you?" a voice I thankfully recognised. "Hi Jack, this is Bobby Hawley on Pilgrim, I've got a spot of bother". I told my story and gave him my position, adding that the police needed Informing. "Leave it with me Bobby, I'll get the Dartmouth inshore lifeboat launched and have the police accompany them. Should be with you within the hour". "Great" I said," I owe you one". Jack was a local Dartmouth lad who I had known for years and was himself a boater, be it a fishing vessel. He was utterly reliable and good at his job, so I returned on deck to consider my next move.

Someone had to cut the body free so I grabbed another line from the cockpit locker, tied off one end to the aft starboard cleat, re-attached my lifeline and went back into the water. I could barely see at all by now but it was still light enough to tie the line around the body to prevent it from returning to the deep. Now for the hard bit; I cut the remainder of the bag to free it from the boat so that I could tackle the prop, and in doing that, it freed the rudder. I came up for some air before going back down to tackle the prop.

Visibility had now deteriorated to the point that I was making no headway, so I returned to the boat to switch on the navigation lights while I waited for the lifeboat's arrival. They would have a waterproof torch on board which would make my task a lot easier.

The VHF broke the sound of the gentle slapping of the waves against the boat's hull "Pilgrim, Pilgrim, Pilgrim, this is the Dartmouth inshore lifeboat, do you read, over"? I scrambled down the companion way steps and grabbed the transceiver; "Dartmouth lifeboat, this is Pilgrim, over"; "Pilgrim, we have you in sight; can we raft alongside, over"? "Come alongside my port side and I'll tie you off". The lifeboat, a rigid bottomed inflatable RIB with a powerful outboard motor approached at speed and I could make out five people on board; four crew members and I assumed a police officer. As they got closer, I could make out the coxswain, Charley Bembridge, a couple of other lads I recognised from the town, one clad in a wetsuit, and one Detective Sergeant Bill Morgan, locally known as 'Morgan', an enormous man with hands the size of dinner plates, and a no nonsense and sometimes over-brutal application of the law, a trait handed down from his strict miner's son upbringing in the South Wales valleys. As the RIB drew alongside, one of the crew threw a line which I attached to the aft port cleat.

"Hi Bobby, got yourself in a spot of bother have we?" came the usually jovial comment from Charley; "not nearly as much bother as that poor soul in the body bag below" was my reply. DS Morgan stood to introduce himself just as the sea decided to rock the boat, and how he managed to avoid a fully clothed dip in the water I don't know, for if he had gone in, we would have been in danger of having both boats swamped. He gathered his balance and composure, held out his hand "I'm DS Morgan and you must be the younger Bobby Hawley. I know your father Robert very well, and what a character your grandfather, Sir James was. He crossed my desk a few times I can tell you, liked getting into trouble, but everybody loved him". "Pleased to meet you Sir" came my reply, my hand numb from a vice like handshake.

"So what's the current situation, have you managed to sort out your underwater problems "asked Charley". I've managed to free the rudder and the bulk of the bag is roped to the starboard aft cleat. I could do with a hand to free the prop as the light faded before I could finish the job". DS Morgan was keen to ensure that as much evidence remained with the body, so it was decided that Ben, our wet-suited lifeboat man would get in the water with me to gently pull the bag close to the RIB. I uncleated the line I had attached to the bag and handed it down to DS Morgan before getting into the water. We slowly moved the bag towards the RIB whilst they took up the slack on the line.

It floated OK presumably because the body was bloated, but it proved to be a four man job to haul it into the RIB. On board the lifeboat, Ben had a 'Spare Air' kit, a type of mini diver's tank and an underwater light which made the task of removing the remaining material from the prop easier. We were back on board in no time.

The crew had secured the body in the RIB, but not before the most junior member of the crew had heaved his dinner up, doing a great job of chumming the water in the process. The lifeboat was just about ready to take off giving me enough time to start the engine, briefly engage forward and reverse to make sure the boat was good to go. DS Morgan asked if I would call in the station in the morning to make a brief statement, and I thanked Charley and the crew for their assistance, untied their line and watched as they pulled away and headed back towards the mouth of the Dart. I dried myself off below and put some warm clothes on before returning on deck.

The return trip to the dock was gladly uneventful, and as I was now thirstier than ever, two hours later than I had planned, I decided to tie up to the town dock for the night, which would allow me to sink at least a couple of pints. The Royal Castle Hotel was one of my favourite watering holes and the food was dammed good there too. It was still busy in the bar even though the big old Grandfather clock was edging 11 o'clock. I ordered my pint at the bar and found a quiet window seat overlooking the inner harbour. I was just beginning to relax after my ordeal when the door opened and in walked a beautiful young lady who I knew very well, but really didn't want to see tonight. I tried desperately to avoid her gaze, but it was me she was scanning the room for, and made a beeline for my table. "Hi Bobby" came the bubbly voice I had known since school days, "just the man I've been looking for", loud enough for everyone in the bar to swing around and gawk. "Aren't you going to buy the girl of your dreams a drink then"?

Julie Fairbrother was a journalist with the local press, the Dartmouth Breeze, but that was her day job, having successfully written several books about Dartmouth's rich history and many of its colourful characters, including my own ancestors who had graced the town for centuries. She was a vodka red-bull girl, which probably explained her ebullient nature, but I liked her a lot. "So, what have you been up to tonight then Bobby" came the inevitable question, delivered just as my mother would have when I had been a naughty little boy, and she knew it. I guessed from her tone that she already knew the answer to her question.

"I've just had a great day out on the boat, and I was hoping for a quiet couple of pints to round off a perfect day until you came in". "Nasty, nasty, now I know your day didn't end perfectly because I saw the lifeboat come in ahead of you". "What makes you think the lifeboat had anything to do with me" I retorted"? "I saw it go out and drove up to the castle for a better view, so before you spin me any more yarns, I also know Bill Morgan was on board, so I guessed it was more than a routine exercise".

It took four pints of Doom Bar before I finally broke, but when I did, I spilt the whole can of beans.

We left The Castle well after midnight and headed back to the town dock. I invited her aboard Pilgrim for a nightcap and climbed over the rail, went to hold out a hand to help her aboard and found she'd turned and disappeared into the darkness, leaving me realising I had just been had, big time. She was a slippery one I thought, but just as well as I would have to move Pilgrim off the town dock before six o'clock in the morning, otherwise Sam, the harbour master would have my 'guts for garters'. So I retired to my bunk and crashed out.

Chapter 2

The alarm woke me at five thirty just as the dawn was breaking. I quickly dressed, grabbed a mug of tea and went up on deck. Even at this early hour, the town was coming to life and there was activity on the river, with a sailboat heading for the open sea on the high tide and a small fishing boat leaving the pontoon. I started the diesel, released the forward and aft spring lines, gave her a little nudge off the dock and jumped on-board. It was slack high tide so we moved away without any problems and headed upriver.

Sand Quay Marina was home to one half of my family's business, which included boat building in two vast sheds, dry dock facilities, a chandlery, and the Dart's favourite riverside restaurant, Smugglers Landing. The waterfront at Sand Quay had always been the home of the Dart's largest boat builder, especially during World War II when the yard built numerous minesweepers, frigates and lightships for the Royal Navy. As D-day approached, many landing craft were built, and with hundreds of vessels anchored in the Dart, repair work became increasingly important.

After the war, the yard reverted to recreational boats and my Grandfather was instrumental in designing and building luxury sailing vessels, first wooden schooners, then steel, and he was one of the earliest to adopt the new "plastic" or "GRP", glass reinforced plastic construction. Both my Grandfather, and later my Father concentrated on the top end of the market, both in luxury sailing and motor yachts, all built and customised to order, and now the 'Blue Dart' marques were highly sought after by the super-rich in Europe, the Middle East and America.

'Pilgrim' had been my Grandfather's own boat, a 54 foot cutter rigged centre-cockpit ketch with every modern 'bang and whistle' added, including fully furled main and mizzen sails, electric winches and windlasses, the latest electronics and communications equipment and wonderfully luxurious accommodation in three separate state rooms. She was also the sleekest looking vessel on the Dart with her lines admired from Monte-Carlo to Miami. When my Grandfather died last year, the Devon business assets passed on to my father Robert, and the Hawley Merchant Bank in the City of London, which it is said was set up originally to effectively launder the ill-gotten gains of privateering, along with the Greenwich Mansion was inherited by his brother Nathan. Half of all the 'assets' were still controlled by my grandmother, with a substantial inheritance for all the grandchildren. He also endowed gifts, which in my case was my beloved 'Pilgrim, which he wanted me to have in memory of the many hours we had spent together on the water. Every time I stepped on to the dock, I could not hide my pride in owning such a beautiful boat, and the memories of such wonderful times I spent in his company filled me with joy, tinged with the sadness of his passing.

I was just starting to hose down the deck and hull to remove the salt from yesterday's sail when my father's dock master, Dave Parsons sauntered over. "Morning Bobby, you're up and about early on a Saturday morning" he said. "Hi Dave, I didn't quite make it back last night, had a spot of bother". "So I hear, the bush telegraph still works around here you know. Even your father's heard the news, he was down here earlier taking Blackie and Barney", our two black Labrador's "for their constitutional and asked after you". "Oh well, saves me telling him the story I suppose. I'd better get finished off here and get cleaned up, they'll be expecting me for breakfast. Thanks for letting me know Dave". "Oh, by the way, there was a chap hanging around here last night looking for you too, foreign fellow, lurking around in the shadows he was, making out he was checking out the boats, but I think he was looking for Pilgrim. Didn't leave his name, said he'd catch up with you".

I finished up and left the boat 'shipshape and Bristol fashion', unplugged one of the golf buggies used to get around the marina and set off up to the house. I drove through the marina and Smuggler's Landing car park then made a detour past the building where the new 'Blue Dart 120' motor yacht was close to launch, around to the North end of the yard where in the smaller building, the three models of sailboat, the 'Regatta 42, 54 and 65' were at various stages of construction. The road then passed under Brunel's Dart Railway, before the private drive to the Hall forked left up through Long Wood, before emerging onto a tree lined avenue with the house, majestic in the early morning sun came into view.

Ancestors dating back to the 14th century had built Hawley Hall high on the forested hill overlooking the river Dart, with views south to the mouth of the river and north towards Totnes. John Hawley had been a privateer of note whose fleet of ships would attack French and Spanish merchantmen in the English Channel. His fortune made, he acquired a vast estate on the Dart's eastern bank and eventually became a respected businessman and Mayor of the town. His body lies in a tomb at Dartmouth's St. Saviour's church. Hawley Hall has been the family home all through the generations and was almost entirely rebuilt in the Georgian era by my Great Grandfather. The estate shrank over the years as pockets of land were sold for housing and farmsteads. Following my Grandfather's death, my father, Sir Robert and my mother Isabelle, my Grandmother, Dame Beatrice, along with my elder brother Tim and younger sister Pippa are privileged to call Hawley Hall our home.

I took the buggy around to the rear courtyard and bounded in through the kitchen entrance where I knew Mrs Harman, our long standing and lovely housekeeper would have something nice for me to pinch before breakfast. She and her husband Brian had the small cottage behind the stables and were both treated like members of the family. Brian was the gardener but also our handyman. The smell of freshly baked bread hit me as soon as I opened the door, and I realised that I had virtually had nothing to eat since midday the day before. She turned and gave me one of her familiar smiles; "Bobby, trust you to smell the food before it's ready, and where have you been, your father's been looking for you for hours"? "You know me Mrs H, here and there, what have you got that'll tie me over until breakfast, I'm ravenous"? "There's some nice little bacon and cheese pastries just out of the oven, how about one of those"? So I gave her one of my cheeky little grins and took two. "Greedy greedy," I heard her mutter as I made for the door. "Thank you Mrs H".

My bedroom was on the second floor with a great view downriver. Although the house was Georgian in style, it had been modernised throughout and all seven bedrooms had their own luxurious bathrooms. I showered and changed before returning downstairs to join the family for breakfast. I breezed in through the open door, "morning all" I chirped, nearly causing my grandmother, who had her back to me to spill her tea. "Morning Bobby" came the four replies almost simultaneously. My sister Pippa was now based in London as a freelance musician, having graduated from the Royal Academy of Music, and was not expected until later in the week. I sat next to my grandmother and gave her a little peck on the cheek. "Another beautiful summer's day" said my father, "how was the river this morning"? "Smooth as a millpond" I said. "You've been out on the river this morning?" asked my mother incredulously, knowing how much I liked my bed. "All night more like" my mischievous brother added. "So what did happen yesterday then"? said my father, "and before you ask, I heard some of the story from the night security chap at the yard whose brother was one of the lifeboat crew". "That explains why half the yard know" I laughed. So I filled the gaps for them, leaving out the most gruesome detail. The dining room had a glorious view of the river past the upper ferry and down Dartmouth's North Embankment to the town jetty, beyond Bayard's Cove, where the

Pilgrim Father's made an unscheduled stop to make repairs before their final landfall in Plymouth on their way to the New World, and as far as Warfleet Creek.

On this wonderful morning, the French doors were open onto the terrace, and a warm summer breeze wafted in. The river was awash with boats of all descriptions with both the rowers and the sailors getting ready for the first day of the Royal Regatta on Thursday. "Bobby, have you replied to the invitation to the Grand Regatta Ball yet, I have it on good authority that this year's event is going to be very special indeed"? asked my mother.

The Regatta Ball is the event of the year, when the 'great and the good' from the local area and special guests from the world of politics, entertainment and sport, to mention just a few, attend the glitziest event of the Regatta at Langham House, a majestic Palladian mansion on the Dart's western bank, and home to the Gilbert family, just a short distance upriver from Hawley Hall. We could see the preparations well underway from the terrace with marquee's adorning the manicured formal gardens. Although I would never admit it publicly, I secretly looked forward to the event each year because it was the rare occasion these days when I could spend the evening close to the love of my life, the Lady Elizabeth. "Not yet" I replied, knowing what was coming next. "So who will be your guest this year

Bobby?" I think that I should escort you Grandma" came my cheeky reply. "Don't you fret about me my boy, I'm being escorted by no less than the Lord of the Manor himself, besides I'm sure you have a string of young ladies begging for an invite". "Maybe I shall escort Pippa then". "Already spoken for" my mother quickly added, "she's bringing down some orchestral conductor chap from London on Wednesday, conducts the BBC Symphony Orchestra by all accounts". "Well you will all have to wait and see. What about you Tim, or is that a silly question"? My brother had been expected to announce his engagement for some time, but the young lady in question was playing very hard to get. "I may surprise you yet little brother" he said with a real twinkle in his eye and an even more mischievous look on his face, he clearly wasn't giving anything away, I checked the time and took my leave, "I'm afraid I must hurry on as I have a previous engagement with a certain DS Morgan at the police station. See you all later", and with that, I excused myself and went back to my room to fetch my phone and car keys.

Chapter 3

I joined the traffic waiting for the upper ferry and regretted using the car. I should have realised that there would be terrible queues on a Saturday in August, and parking in town would not be pleasant either. I've never tired of crossing the Dart and today was even better with all the activity on the river, little dinghy sailboats weaving and tacking their way up and down river, rowers out in their whalers coupled with the regular pleasure craft mingling with ferries and river trips, the whistle of the Dartmouth Steam Railway making its way toward Kingswear station, a feast of colour on both banks, and on the river itself. Lady luck was with me as I managed to park my Range Rover almost outside the police station.

A tap on the intercom, and my name was all that was needed, the door buzzed allowing me to enter. The desk Sergeant greeted me, I had seen him many times around the town. "You're famous Mr Hawley" he said, "I've policed this town for the last twenty years, and never managed to get my picture on the front page of the local"! I had no idea what he was on about, but he shuffled this morning's copy of the Breeze across the desk and there I was, top story by non-other than Julie Fairbrother, with a half page picture of me on-board Pilgrim. The bitch, I thought, she really did roll me over last night.

Just as I was contemplating how I would get even with her, a non-too pleased DS Morgan appeared. He showed me into the interview room whereupon I found out how displeased he really was with my indiscretion, and lectured me for a good fifteen minutes on how police work required a degree of confidentiality, especially serious crime such as a murder investigation. He then handed me a blank pad and asked me for a detailed statement in my own words, offered me tea or coffee which I declined, and left the room. The statement was brief but contained the order of events, and having read it, he asked me to sign and date the document. His demeanour changed and he became more approachable again, so I felt able to ask him if the body had revealed any clues as to its identity? He said that as they had no facilities in Dartmouth, the body had been left largely undisturbed and sent immediately to the Devon and Cornwall Police HQ at Exeter for a post-mortem. He did add that the investigation would be much more difficult as both hands had been severed, which shocked me, so no fingerprints would be available, but DNA evidence should still aid identification of the body, but it would just take longer. He passed me his card and said that I was to contact him directly if anything else came to light. He offered me his hand which I sheepishly took and I left the police station nursing a throbbing hand once more.

Julie lived above her dad's bookshop in Lower Street, so I left the car and walked over past the inner harbour and went into the shop. "Hi Mr Fairbrother, do you know if Julie's in"? "Come in Bobby, Julie said you'd probably come in this morning, cracking piece in the Breeze aye? Should make the 'nationals' tomorrow with a bit of luck lad". "The 'nationals'? What do you mean, the 'nationals' sir"? "Oh, she submits the most interesting news to The Mail, Times, Telegraph and the like, and trivial stuff to the 'red tops', so you might be even more famous tomorrow morning". That's all I needed, if DS Morgan was already annoyed with me today, he would be well pissed off when he choked over his corn flakes tomorrow morning. "Where is Julie, is she in the flat"? "No, she's not back yet, she took the dog for its usual walk this morning and I haven't seen her since. She's normally back by now, what time is it"? "It's a quarter to twelve" I replied. "She's never this long, come to think of it, we never had our coffee together today". I took out my mobile and tried calling her but it went straight into voicemail, so I left a message asking her to call me. "Where does she normally go with the dog"? "She heads for the castle and walks part of the coastal path, but she's always back before eleven". Now he sounded concerned, so I reassured him that I would find her and headed back to the car for the short drive to the castle.

I managed to park and was just about to head for the path when I spotted Julie's dog, a Retriever called Rusty, who was being pampered with some cake by a couple of tourist. I walked over and the dog instantly recognised me and came bounding over." Come on Rusty", I called, made a fuss of him and stuck my head in the Castle Tea Room, but there was no sign of Julie either inside or on the terrace, so I asked one of the waitresses if she had seen her? "I thought that was Rusty, we often see Julie, but not this morning, she must have been here before we opened" she said. I took Rusty with me and walked along the path down to Castle Cove, then Sugary Cove and as far as Ladies Cove via Deadmans Cove, but there was no sign of her either on or close to the path, or God forbid, down on the rocks below.

I was just about to retrace my steps when my mobile rang, it was Julie, very distraught, sobbing uncontrollably and unable to get her words out. "Slow down and tell me where you are and I'll come and get you". It took a short while before she calmed down and was able to tell me that she had been dumped out of a car on the edge of town, she thought it was close to the sewage works by the woods. I told her not to worry and raced the dog back to the car. I headed towards the top of town and dropped down to Townstal Wood, and within ten minutes saw Julie just visible on the edge of Norton Wood, hiding from someone who had clearly frightened her. I stopped the car and walked over to her. She was crying bitterly, tears running down her blotchy face and trembling. I put my arms around her and hugged her tightly to me, trying to reassure her that everything was alright. It wasn't until she saw Rusty's wagging tail in the back of the car that she stopped trembling, and wiping her tears, she climbed into the car and gave the old dog such a big hug. "What happened Julie, who brought you here, and what has he done to you"? "Take me home, Booby, I just want to go home", so I drove her home mostly in silence. I stopped outside the shop and she was out of the car almost before it had come to a halt, she was in through the shop door with Rusty close behind before I had a chance to say anything.

  I decided to park the car again and went back to the bookshop, but found the door locked and a closed sign hanging in the window. I knocked on the flat door and eventually Julie's father came down, "she's pretty upset at the moment Bobby, so go gentle on her". We went back upstairs and found Julie sat in her living room drinking the mug of tea her dad had made her. She looked a little more like the girl I'd known since school days, normally feisty and seemingly never ruffled by anything, but clearly whatever happened this morning had scared the living daylights out of her. I sat down on the couch next to her, put my arm around her and just calmly asked if she wanted to tell me what happened. She said nothing at first, but bit by bit, she told us that she was going through the wood towards the castle when a car pulled up and a man bundled her into the back seat, and the driver sped off up the lane. She struggled in vain as the man pulled a hood over her head. He threatened her that unless she remained quiet and stopped struggling, he would hurt her. They drove for about ten minutes before they stopped, dragged her out of the car, and with one either side of her, marched her over some rough ground and sat her down on what felt like a tree stump. She said that the man who spoke had a foreign accent, but his English was very perfect. He told her that as long as she told him the truth they would not harm her. It was all to do with the story in the Breeze, and me. They wanted to know how much she knew, whether there was anything not printed, especially if the police had identified the body, and whether I had told her everything. "I tried to pull the hood off my head but they roughed me up a bit, grabbed me by the throat and warned me that unless I stopped, I would also face a watery grave. He warned me not to go to the police or tell anyone, because they would find me. Next thing, they told me to lie face down, close my eyes and not move for five minutes if I wanted to live". They removed the hood, warned her again not to open her eyes, and she heard them disappear through the wood, two car doors slam shut and the car drive away.

I tried to ask Julie some of the many questions going through my head, but she was adamant that she neither knew anything else nor did she see either of the men. When I mentioned going to the police, she almost became hysterical and told me to leave. I tried to reassure her, but she begged me not to tell anyone, so I left the two of them and walked down to the embankment and sat wondering what the hell I should do. Why would whoever had killed my 'body in a bag' break cover, when they knew that identification would be difficult at best without fingerprints, and what would a foreigner be up to in Dartmouth that had already got one person killed? Was it the same person Dave had seen lurking around the yard?

Chapter 4

The ministerial Jaguar and its police escort were winding their way through the narrow Devon lanes, on the last leg of the journey from Whitehall to Langham House. In the back seat, working on some ministerial papers was The Rt. Hon. Edward Gilbert MP, Secretary of State for the Foreign and Commonwealth Office, and the local Member of Parliament for the Totnes constituency. The parliamentary summer recess saw an exodus of MP's from London to their country homes in August, and after a particularly difficult year at the Foreign Office, he was looking forward to spending more time with his family, especially his father, the Earl of Langham, Lord William Gilbert, or just plain old Daddy to the family, who was still mourning the loss of his wife, the Countess Elizabeth eighteen months earlier.

The car swung in through the gates of Langham and drove up the tree lined gravel drive to the house, where he unexpectedly saw the industry taking place on the terrace and garden, with hoards of workmen putting up marquees, lighting and all the paraphernalia associated with the forthcoming Regatta Grand Summer Ball. He'd forgotten how much work his father and brother put into the event each year and he could see that this years' was going to be bigger and better than ever. He also had a mighty surprise for them which he would announce later at dinner, when other members of the family would have arrived. He got out of the car, and as he approached the steps leading to the ornate front entrance, he caught a glimpse of his elder brother Michael who was dispensing instructions and organising the workforce as he always did. "Hey Michael, how the devil are you"? "Ted, trust you to turn up when most of the hard graft's done"! They embraced, patted each other on the back and walked towards the doors leading from the terrace to the dining hall, with Michael continuing to dish out instructions as they went. Other household staff were unpacking boxes of crockery, glasses, cutlery and a myriad of items required to feed and entertain at least five hundred guests at next week's ball. "How is the old man, is he still brooding around the place and drinking too much"? asked Ted. "You won't recognise him" came Michael's reply, "he's acting like a teenager, when he's here that is, because we hardly see him these days. He spends most of his time at the golf club, or so he tells us! He's always out to dinner, and you probably know that he spent the whole of last month at the St. Tropez villa. I swear he's up to something and I'm sure it's a woman". Ted was speechless and intrigued, the last time he was down at Whitsun, he was very withdrawn and very difficult to communicate with. "I don't believe you, I'm going to have to see this with my own eyes, where is he"? I told you, he's never here, I saw him leave an hour ago all dressed up so you can bet he's entertaining. I know he's expecting you and I heard him say he's booked dinner for us all at Taylor's in Dartmouth tonight at eight, so he'll be back late afternoon I expect".

Michael led the way into the conservatory where his beautiful wife Ellen was arranging a most glorious vase of summer flowers from the garden. "Hello Ted, I saw your car turn up. You're looking very dapper, High Office must be suiting you". Ellen was the most elegant woman Ted had ever known, even in her gardening clothes she looked as if she had come straight off the catwalk. She was certainly a flower of Devon, born across the moor in Tavistock, and descended from no other than Sir Francis Drake. Her lineage was pure Devon, pure English and pure Aristocracy. She was one beautiful woman who turned heads wherever she went. "Hello Ellen, you look radiant as usual, I don't know how you do it". Michael and Ellen had three children, the eldest, George was undoubtedly helping with the preparations for Regatta events as he was chairman of the organising committee, an avid sailor and a 'chip off the old block', so much like his Grandfather. "Is my favourite niece here yet"? "No, Elizabeth is due in Totnes on the six o'clock train so she'll be in time for our dinner tonight. Did Michael tell you that Daddy's organised dinner in town"? "I've heard the news, and frankly I can't wait to see the miraculous transformation I've been hearing about" said Ted.

"Now where's that Ricky, has he been behaving himself lately"? Ricky was their youngest, and a handful, always in trouble with the police for fighting, drunkenness and womanising. Many an angry boyfriend or husband had left Ricky laid out cold, only for the police to bring him home in the back of their car in the middle of the night. He was certainly turning into the "black sheep" of the family, and the only one who could get through to him at all was Elizabeth, and since she was now based at London's Imperial College, Ted had heard he'd fallen further off the rails. Michael pulled a face; "sore point I'm afraid" he said, "I've tried everything with him, gave him a position at the plant which I think he deliberately messed up. We're both pulling our hair out, even Daddy has had strong words with him, threatening to cut off his inheritance unless he bucked up his ideas, but to no avail, all he did was disappear for two whole weeks. So for now, we've given up on him, and hope that Elizabeth can help put him straight over the holidays.

The Langham Estate was one of the largest landowners in Devon after the Duchy of Cornwall and the National Trust, with thousands of acres of grade one arable land split up into about twenty farmsteads, all paying rent. It was also a very diverse business with apple orchards feeding the Devon Red cider mill, a vineyard producing some of the best quality English wines, and a salmon fishery and smokehouse on the banks of the Dart producing top quality fish for the country's best restaurants. The main business however was a throwback to the days of pioneering, privateering and even pirating, the business of providing armaments for the Royal Navy. Eventually the factories diversified and started developing and building planes for the Navy and the RAF during both world wars from their factories in Plymouth. With the ever-changing technology of modern warfare, the Earl had formed longstanding relationships with the Scientific and Electronics departments at his old University at Cambridge, and the Mechanical Engineering experts at the local Exeter University, which ensured that the plant embraced the needs of the twenty first century. As a result, they were at the forefront in the design and manufacture of drones in the UK, with demand for both the Skykite, capable of deploying hellfire missiles, and the smaller Skylark drone used for observation and eavesdropping, off the charts both in Europe and the USA, driven by the ever increasing war on terrorism. Michael was now at the helm and the business was thriving and in safe hands for at least the current and next generation with George fully immersed in the business.

"Go and freshen up Ted, and when you're ready, join us for some drinks in the garden and we can catch up some more. You never know, Daddy may have graced us with his presence by then" said Michael, raising his eyebrows at the same time.

Ricky downed the last dregs of his lager, said his farewells to the group of friends, paying special attention to one pretty girl with a quick grope of her bottom, and left the Dartmouth Arms before she could retaliate. "See you all later at The George", he called out, a favourite hangout with live music on weekends featuring local groups. He made his way along the embankment towards the town jetty where he had docked The Lady Elizabeth's tender earlier in the day. He spotted me sat on the bench by the steps to the dock, came up behind and whacked me on the back with such force that I nearly jumped straight into the water. "Hi Bobby, seen any more dead bodies lately"? Ricky was always full of high spirits, full of fun, and I enjoyed his company. He was two years younger and had tried every which way to get my sister Pippa into his bed, but of course she would have none of it, and had outwitted him so many times he had gracefully given up with the largest bunch of red roses ever delivered to the hall as a peace offering and parting gift. "What are you up to Ricky", knowing full well, having had a whiff of his breath that he had just crawled out of the pub. "Been summoned home" he said, "the whole bloody family's arriving for the summer holidays today, so I've got to behave myself". "Has Elizabeth arrived"? I asked, trying not to sound too excited. "Still got the hots for my big sis then Bobby" came his reply with a wink of his eye, and he staggered towards the dock steps, "picking her up off the six o'clock train" he said, "and if you just happen to be at the right place at the right time, you might catch a glimpse of her at Taylors tonight at eight".

With that, he jumped into the tender, started the engine, untied the lines and took off from the dock, rocking the other boats with his wake. Unlucky for Ricky, the Harbour Master was just idling up the river, pulled him over, and promptly gave him a ticket for breaking the six knot speed limit. Everyone liked Ricky except the authorities it would seem, his high spirits always landing him in trouble.

I decided to follow his lead, found the car and headed home. I rarely went to the hall before checking in at the marina, and as I turned the corner, I spotted the new Regatta 65 in the water being rigged. The main mast had already been stepped and the crane was still supporting it whilst the rigging crew secured the shrouds. Even with only one mast in place she really was a looker, with her sleek dark blue hull and red boot stripe just above the waterline. Once she was rigged, she would undergo a sea trial before taking her place on the mooring alongside the new Blue Dart 120 Motor yacht for the duration of the Regatta, whilst invited and prospective customers would be ferried out for viewings. The marina and yard was a hive of activity with the day sailors and some early arrivals for the coming weeks' events berthing up.

    I was already excited at the prospect of seeing Elizabeth, so I hurried up to the hall and showered and changed for the evening.

Chapter 5

Michael was striding back up the long walk from the dock to the house. There was no sign of Ricky anywhere and he wasn't answering his phone either which infuriated him even more. Ricky's car was still parked behind the house but the tender was missing from the dock. Surely he hadn't decided to pick Elizabeth up in the boat because Steamer Quay was a fair walk from Totnes Station and Ricky wasn't known for walking very far to anywhere, besides, knowing Elizabeth, she would have enough luggage to sink the boat! He stormed back into the house in a dark mood, Ellen was in the kitchen with George who had returned from his preparations for the sailing events. He was hungry as usual and as cook had been given the evening off, Ellen had made him a sandwich. She heard Michael call her name, "in here darling, George is home", he walked into the room with the look of thunder, "that bloody boy is nowhere to be seen, I expect he's still in town, probably in the pub because the tender is missing from the dock". "I doubt he's in town Dad, I saw him leave and head up river, that is until the harbour master gave him a ticket for speeding", George gave one of his guttural chuckles, "but he carried on and by the time I looked again he was past the ferry". "Where the hell is he then, it's five thirty and he's supposed to pick Elizabeth up at the station at six. I expect the bugger's called in at the Ferry Boat Inn and lost all track of time". He telephoned the FBI, as it was locally known, but the barmaid said they hadn't seen him all day, which she admitted was unusual. "I don't expect they'd tell me even if he was there, I'll box his bloody ears when I see him". George offered to pick up Elizabeth, much to his father's relief. "Take the Bentley if you like" he said, but George wisely took his own Range Rover because he knew too that Elizabeth did not travel light!

Hawley Hall was deserted by the time I emerged from a light snooze and a long shower. My father and mother had been invited to a Gala Dinner at the Grand Hotel in Torquay to mark the start of the Torbay Regatta, Grandmother was at a charity event at Dartington Hall and Tim had presumably gone off somewhere for the evening with his "catch me if you can" lady friend. It was after seven and I was undecided whether to take one of the marina tenders or the car, but it being August, a Saturday night, police with breathalysers and virtually impossible parking, I decided the boat was the better option, grabbed a warm coat, for it could get chilly on the water later, jumped in the buggy and headed down to the marina.

It was heaving there too with Smugglers Landing restaurant packed to the gunnels and the visitor pontoons rafted three deep. There wasn't much space on the jetty either but I managed to tie up without having to hop from one dinghy to the other to get onto the pontoon. I headed for the Royal Castle having suddenly realised that I'd had nothing to eat since breakfast, and it would also serve as the perfect spot to see Elizabeth arrive being only a few doors up the street. The Galleon Bar was a sea of locals and visitors and they were three deep at the bar. Being a regular and a good tipper has its advantages and my customary pint of Doom Bar was being pulled whilst the barmaid served another man. When they were busy, which was most of the time, they tabbed up my bill for me to settle later so I managed to order a medium Rib Eye with all the trimmings when I picked up my drink. It was still early for any of my friends to be in so I managed to eat my food in peace and quiet, until that was, half the sailing club came in through the door. They were certainly in high spirits after a day on the water, then a couple of the lads spotted me, "hey, come and join us Bobby and tell us how the 'burial at sea' business is going"! They were always ribbing each other, everything was a joke but they were great fun and I had spent many happy hours competing with them on the water. "I don't do burials, I'm only involved in the resurrection business" I chirped, which got me a laugh and cost me a round of drinks.

I saw the Bentley come round the embankment which was my cue to make my escape, I settled my tab and timed my exit perfectly just as Elizabeth was getting out of the car. "Fancy bumping into you here Bobby" she said, and walked towards me beaming. We had fallen in love as children and were utterly relaxed in each other's company, some saying we were more like brother and sister than most siblings. Her father, who had always treated me with respect did not like the closeness of our relationship and suspected that there was more to it than met the eye! I embraced her and gave her a peck on both cheeks. "I don't have to ask how you are" I said, "you look absolutely stunning", she was a younger version of her mum, Ellen, and I was so happy to see her again. She turned to her family who were waiting to go into Taylor's, "you go ahead, I'll be just a few minutes", so they went in but I could tell that they did not entirely approve. "If I know you Bobby, this isn't entirely a coincidence is it"? "I hate to admit it, Ricky gave me the heads-up earlier this afternoon". "He's in big trouble, he was supposed to pick me up from the station but he's gone AWOL again". "I'm surprised, he left the dock in the tender in plenty of time to get to your train". "Dad swears he couldn't pass the FBI without going in so he's probably legless by now, he was supposed to be having dinner with us, anyway, I mustn't keep them waiting any longer, will I see you in church tomorrow morning"? "Of course" I replied, although I hadn't been to church since she was home at Whitsun. With that, she was gone, and I had that empty feeling again.

I didn't think for one minute that Ricky would risk being seen in town, but if he was going to be anywhere, he'd be in the George. I fancied a little live music so I sauntered up the embankment, stuck my head through the Floating Bridge pub door, not really expecting to find him there and carried on towards the George. I don't know why, but something was giving me an uneasy feeling, probably because of all the family, Elizabeth was his 'guardian angel', the one he would run to if he'd hurt himself when he was a child or, as was often the case, he'd been a naughty boy, and she would always defend him when their parents would most likely have been less lenient. For Ricky to not go and pick her up from the station, something pretty important had got in the way.

I could hear the music coming from the George's beer garden, a good old Reggae band tonight and it sounded like one of my favourites, the Barefoot Bandits from Exmouth. It was still quite early but the pub was already busy, mostly visitors but also a lot of the local crowd were in and I spotted the friends he hung out with through the door to the garden, but no Ricky. I went up to the bar and decided on a pint of Devon Red cider for a change. I spotted some of the lads from the boatyard, including Dave, the marina dock master and joined them at the table. We had all been friends for many years, mainly through work, but they were a great bunch of guys, and although I was their bosses' son, they treated me no different and we all had a great laugh together. As Bob Marley's 'I shot the sheriff' rang out, we were all in a party mood and the drinks flowed to the point where I had more than mellowed out and was beginning to stagger.

A group of girls on holiday had joined us and we were all having a great time jigging around to the music. By the time Bobby McFerrin's 'Don't worry, be happy' came round, I had all but forgotten about Ricky's problems and was doing my level best to get off with a girl called Jennifer, a task that proved to be harder than winning the lottery, and resulted in a good old ribbing from the rest of the lads.

It must have been well past one o'clock before we dragged ourselves out of the George and they were still taking the piss as we headed back towards the harbour singing Bob Marley's 'No Woman, No Cry'. I knew they would all remind me of tonight for years and it would be the source of banter at the yard for some time. I was unsteady on my feet going down the steps to the jetty and I had never realised before how precarious it was to walk along a floating pontoon in the dark when you're as drunk as a lord! I managed to get into the tender without making an ass of myself even though they were all howling and willing me to fall into the water. "Steady as she goes, Bobby and if you should see a mermaid on your way home, check her name's not Jennifer before you chat her up".

The howls of laughter receded as I concentrated on manoeuvring the boat off the dock without drawing any more attention to myself, and I safely headed up-river. It is surprising how a chill wind concentrates the mind and in no time I was approaching Sand Quay. As I sobered a little, that pang of guilt came back to me and I still worried as to whether Ricky was OK. It was only a ten minute jaunt up the river to Dittisham and the Ferry Boat Inn so even though it was dark, I knew the river well and decided to check out whether Elizabeth's father's theory was correct. I had no idea what I thought I would achieve but at least I could give Elizabeth some news in the morning. I approached the dock and saw the tender tied up safely. I pulled alongside and although the life jackets were strewn all over the boat, everything seemed in order and I assumed Ricky had drunk a bellyful and crashed out somewhere. I headed back, made my way to the hall and needed no rocking!

Chapter 6

Sunday morning breakfast was a special event at the hall. In addition to the normal bacon and eggs, Mrs Harman made us a big pile of pancakes which I especially loved with fresh raspberries, Greek yogurt and honey. "You'll get fat as a barrel with all those pancakes Bobby, I don't know where you put it"? "I'm still a growing lad Grandma, and Mrs Harman's pancakes are something else, pity to waste them seeing Tim doesn't have any, him being fat already"! That comment got the clump around the head from my brother that I deserved.

The family were in good spirits this morning and my head was remarkably good considering the pounding I had given it last night. My mother was full of stories from their dinner in Torquay and she had apparently managed to prize my father off his seat to dance more than once which everyone agreed was a minor miracle. Grandma too was in fine fettle given that she was probably considerably poorer following her charity event. Tim, quiet as he was, still had a smirk on his face. He was obviously pleased with himself so I ventured to assume that his secretive love life had blossomed. "So when's the happy day then Tim"? "Well I do have some news" he chirped, "but not the sort you're all expecting". "So you're going to make an honest woman of Frances at long last" said Grandma. "Not exactly" he said and I saw my mother stiffen in anticipation of what was coming next. "She's not........" but before she could ask, Tim cut her off and said, "You won't know this but Frances and I called it a day more than three months ago. We weren't getting on, all she seemed to want to do was party party party and I was getting fed up with it so we parted amicably". I could see my mother was disappointed, Tim was the eldest son and heir, thirty four years of age and still living with mum and dad! "But I do have news which I hope you will approve of, I met a lady whilst I was still with Frances but we both were in relationships then and we didn't see each other again for almost six months. We have been together these past ten or more weeks and we are just so happy". "Who is she, do we know her, is she from a good family........" my mother was getting more excitable by the minute. Tim again cut her off, "that's not all mother, last night, we decided to tell both our families. You know the family well and I'm sure you will approve. Her name is Georgina, in fact, she's the Lady Georgina, daughter of Lord and Lady Fowlkes of Compton, and I have invited her to be my guest at the Regatta Ball, but of course you will meet her before then". Both my father and mother were speechless but I could also see they were delighted with the news. Grandma was the first to say anything, "Timothy, you have yourself quite a catch there, she's a delightful young lady who I met when she attended one of our functions earlier this year". My mother wasn't speechless for long and with tears of delight she gave Tim such a hug. "Should I prepare to buy a new outfit, because I can just see you two walking down the aisle"? "Now don't get ahead of yourself mother, but we are very much in love". "You must invite her over for our garden party on Wednesday, Pippa and her young man will be here by then along with brother Nathan and his family and we can all meet her at the same time".

The Hawley's garden party was 'the' event to mark the start of Regatta week and preparations would be frantic over the next two days with the front lawn transformed into a showcase 'Chelsea' style garden. Half the town was invited and the other half would be attending a fun night of music and dance at Coronation Park, all concluding with a spectacular firework show for which the guests at Hawley would have a fantastic vantage.

Excitement was rising in the Hawley household and the week ahead would prove eventful, but I still had an unease in my stomach, why I did not know. My father, always intensely aware and often able to read minds stood up to leave, "now the Lady Elizabeth is home, I expect you will grace us with your presence in church this morning Bobby," he said with a smirk on his face. "I shall father", and with that, breakfast was over and we all got ready for church.

Father Godfrey greeted the congregation at the historic South door of the ancient St. Saviours Church in Dartmouth. He made a special point of welcoming me back," it's nice to see you again Bobby, don't be such a stranger", which my mother heartily agreed with. Elizabeth and the rest of her family were already sat in their usual pews which were in front and to our right so I was unable to make eye contact with her, but she did turn around once, saw me and smiled. The service was traditional C of E with a special blessing for the success of the Regatta Week, for which the church and local charities received generous donations. The service ended with a rousing rendition of Hubert Parry's 'I was glad' accompanied by the organ, the choir and the ceremonial trumpeter's of the Royal Britannia Naval College.

As we filed out of church I was desperate to see Elizabeth, and was relieved to see she was making her way over. "Hi Elizabeth, I'd forgotten how much I enjoyed church, but I only ever seem to come when I know you're home". "You are stupid Bobby, we hardly ever get time to talk even when I am home". "Well, let's do something about that, can I see you this afternoon"? "Oh I don't know Bobby, I haven't spent much time with my family lately and Daddy will wonder where I am, especially since Ricky's still not come home". I told her about finding the tender at the Dittisham dock which put her mind at rest at least and after some persuasion, she agreed to meet me at the boathouse at three o'clock.

Before I had a chance to say anything else I felt a heavy hand on my shoulder, turned and there was DS Morgan, he thrust a copy of The Mail in my hand, opened on page three, and there I was, a picture of me grinning like a Cheshire cat, stood on Pilgrim's deck. I was just about to say something when he produced the Sunday Mirror, "you've gone one better and made the front page in this one, I hope you and your girlfriend are happy now, you've certainly made my superiors angry with me and I'm equally pissed off with you. No more talking to the press 'cause believe you me, with the Regatta this week there will be plenty of them sniffing about. Do I make myself clear"? I thought about telling him to piss off but could see no advantage in annoying him further, so I apologised and was about to remind him that Julie was not my girlfriend when Elizabeth swooned off and DS Morgan turned and marched away. Before I could retrieve the situation my father came over. "What was all that about then Bobby, you seem to have angered both our local police detective and your lady friend without saying much"? "I've made the papers again so he's not happy and I haven't a clue what's upset Elizabeth", but by the time I turned to look for her she was in the car and gone. "Your mother and I are having lunch with the Bradley's and Grandma's invited too, do you want to take the car and drop it off later"?

I declined the offer and walked over to the river where the heats for the rowing events were already in progress. I hadn't stood there for more than five minutes when Julie walked towards me. "You're looking very smart today Mr Hawley, been to repent your sins have you"? "And what sins might I need repenting Miss Fairbrother". "Well I heard the name Jennifer mentioned". "Oh God! What did you hear"? "Nothing much, just a few lads having a laugh in the newsagents this morning, anything newsworthy I can write about for the Breeze"? It was a tongue in cheek comment which I ignored. "I think you've got me into enough trouble for one weekend, DS Morgan collared me again this morning and gave me the third degree"! She laughed and I could see she was back to her jolly self. "You OK now"? I asked. "Rusty missed out on his morning walk today but other than that, I'm fine". "Fancy a cup of coffee, I'd offer you a proper drink but I had a bellyful last night and my head is still pounding".

We headed for the Cafe Alf Fresco to avoid the hordes of tourists at the Station Cafe and sat there for what seemed ages just chatting. "Are you taking anyone special to the ball on Saturday" she asked, and before I could answer, "take me, I'd love to go, I'm sure I'd get a great story for the Breeze with all those celebs there". "You'd be the last person in the world I'd ask, I could just imagine you going round all the tables with your notebook and camera looking for a juicy story". "Oh well, worth a try"! Julie was never more desirable than when she was in a teasing mood, and today I could easily have asked her to be my partner at the ball, but for a reason I didn't even know myself, I held back and the moment passed. We finished our coffees and I made my excuse to leave, we parted and I headed off to catch a lift on the Dittisham Ferry and persuade the captain to drop me off at Sand Quays' outer pontoon which was strictly against company policy.

Although my head had stopped pounding, I had another of those empty feelings and was completely confused with what was going on in my mind. The lads had completely finished rigging the Regatta 65 and all her sails were raised whilst they adjusted the various shroud tensions. She was beautiful, a very elegant cruising sailboat and I would be the first to sail her when she went out for a short sea trial in the morning.

Having changed out of my suit, I was enjoying a glass of beer on the terrace and catching the warm rays of the afternoon sun when I spotted a sleek motor yacht coming upriver. I reached for the binoculars which we always kept handy on the conservatory bookcase and was surprised; I thought for a moment that she was a military vessel visiting Britannia for she was entirely cloaked in a black finish, her hull, decks and superstructure. The only colour on display was the French Tricolour on her stern and the UK and Devon courtesy flags on her starboard aerial mast. She was a good fifty metres in length with three decks, an impressive and powerful looking yacht but strangely I could not see any crew members' on-deck. She passed Sand Quay and carried on upriver and I guessed I would get a closer view of her when I headed for Langham.

    I checked the time and made my way to the marina, I could not help myself, but whenever Elizabeth was home I seemed to be ridiculously early for our liaisons and today was no exception. I took the tender out into the river, there was still a ripple on the water from the yachts' wake and when I turned the bend, there she was picking up a buoy in the deep water channel just below Greenway House, Agatha Christie's former home on the Dart, now owned by the National Trust. I just had to take a closer peek at her. The 'Magie Noir', or 'Black Magic' in English hailed from Marseille, she was a beauty but in a sinister sort of way. Even the crew on the bow were dressed all in black uniforms and all her ports, including her bridge were tinted. She was one impressive boat but why she chose to moor this far up the river when all the Regatta events were between the upper and lower ferries I could not imagine. One of the crew was indicating that I should move away immediately which was not surprising as I had done two full circuits of her hull, so I turned and continued my journey. Galmpton and Stoke Gabriel shone like jewels in the afternoon sun and it wasn't long before Langham's boathouse came into view.

As children, the summer holidays were a magical time for us, and Elizabeth and I had explored every inch of the river in a little row boat, landing at Duncannon Copse and South Downs Wood, played and fished in Mill Pool, creating our very own 'Swallows and Amazons', and we had eventually become lovers. Both our families had forbidden us to see each other but we always managed to outfox them, and continued to meet until we both went away to University. There had been an ongoing feud between the Hawley's and Gilbert's for generations which intensified when our Grandfather's had physically come to blows for the love of my Grandmother. She had eventually chosen to marry into the Hawley clan and the families had continued their hostilities for many years. Thankfully, an uneasy peace had descended and relations had improved with the younger generations, which seemed to have now entered into a new era of warmer friendship.

I tied up the boat and stepped onto the dock, admired the classic Grand Banks Trawler that was the Lady Elizabeth, named after Elizabeth's Grandmother, retrieved the boathouse key from its hiding place and went in. It was small and cosy with a living room with panoramic views of the river perched over the water, a bedroom, bathroom and kitchen. It had at one time been let as a short term holiday home for the many fishermen who came to catch the Dart's Salmon but since fishing restrictions had been imposed it was used very occasionally by the family for the utter peace and quiet it afforded. It was a haven for wildlife with spectacular glimpses of the blue and orange Kingfisher hovering above the water. They kept the kitchen stocked with non-perishables and I found myself a beer and sat at the open window watching the small river craft and ferries pass.

Elizabeth was late as usual and was not her laid back self. She seemed agitated and was clearly uncomfortable, almost unable to look at me. I walked towards her and saw that she had been crying. I tried to embrace her but she pulled away and sat in the window seat. "What's the matter, has something happened"? "Oh Bobby, I shouldn't have come here, I can't do this anymore". "Why Elizabeth, we have loved each other since we were children". "That's just it Bobby, were not children any more, we've both moved on, we lead independent lives miles apart and we only see each other on high days and holidays". "I know that and I miss you so much, but when you come home, my heart misses a beat and I can't wait to be with you again". "But even when I'm home we only see each other in secret because both our families have done everything to keep us apart. When did we last have dinner together or go to a show or just sit on the beach holding hands and eating an ice cream" I was silent because we had never done any of those things, we had played as children and made love in the woods and in this boathouse, but we had never been on a proper date. "That's not normal Bobby, that's not what normal couples do, we never had a chance and now it's too late". "It doesn't have to be, we don't have to cower down to our families, we could go away together and start a fresh life". "On Bobby, my lovely darling Bobby, you would, too, but where would we go and what would we do, your life is here in Dartmouth, your family and the business, your beloved "Pilgrim" and your friends whereas my life and career is in London. We have to move on and cherish that intimate friendship and memories we have had for so many years": "Christ, you sound as if one of us is going to die and we're never going to see each other ever again". It was me now who had tears in my eyes and I had a serious lump in my throat because I knew she was right but I didn't want to admit it. It was Elizabeth who broke the silence, she came to me and we just held each other for what seemed an age. "I love you and will always love you and my heart will always flutter when I see you, but you knew that being apart was bound to break the spell. It took more than twenty five years for it to happen", we both chuckled, "but it was inevitable". I looked at her face, there were tears streaming down her cheeks, I wiped them away and we kissed, a gentle loving kiss that would live with me forever. "You are right and I've known it for a long time, but I was not willing to let you go. I love you so much it hurts and every time we parted, I'd have this awful empty feeling, but I'm glad you've had the courage to say what I never could".

"I'll have that drink you never offered me now" she said and I found a bottle of Langham's own red wine and a couple of glasses and joined her on the sofa. She was still a little pensive and seemed as if she had something else on her mind but was struggling with it, and having accepted that life would not be the same again, I decided to flush it out of her. "So how's life in the big city then, is working at the Imperial College living up to you expectations"? She admitted that she loved the medical research work, it was challenging and very fulfilling. She also loved the social life in the city and had been invited to parties through her Uncle

Ted at the Foreign Office. Eventually she felt relaxed enough to open up. "I do have something I want to tell you Bobby, I've been seeing someone for some time and we have become very close". She stopped, not sure what my reaction would be, but having accepted that our future was to be as friends, I was calmly resolved that she would have other men in her life in London. I said nothing and she continued. "Well, we met at one of Uncle Ted's parties, his name is Anthony and he's asked me to marry him". "Wow, you have moved on a pace, have you said yes"? I could see she was hesitant in case the news proved too much in one go. "I have, and that's not all, he's just been appointed as the next Ambassador and Permanent Representative of the UK Mission to the UN in Geneva, and he wants me to move there with him". "You don't waste any time do you; you'll be telling me you're expecting his baby next"! "Don't be ridiculous Bobby, you should know me better than that". "I thought I did but things are moving so fast my head hasn't stopped spinning. Look, I'm happy for you, I'm just not sure I'm happy for myself, everything has turned upside down in the last hour and it's taking a while to sink in". "You'll be fine, I hear that you've got a girlfriend in town, who is she, do I know her"? "What the hell makes you think that I have a girlfriend"? "It was that policeman at the church this morning". I told her the story about the body and Julie's article; she knew Julie from school days, "why don't you bring her to the ball on Saturday, I'd love to see her again".

We finished our wine, chatting and laughing about old times," I don't think we'll see much of each other now you're going across the channel" I said, "but promise me you won't forget our friendship and please don't feel awkward in my company on those rare occasions we do meet even if your family, and even your intended don't approve". "You are a silly noggin Bobby, I will never forget us and what we've had, you will always be in my heart". She looked at her watch, "I must go or I'll be late for dinner, we have the French Foreign Minister joining us tonight and I believe they are going to the Factory tomorrow. He's officially on holiday but mixing a bit of business with pleasure". "That must be his yacht down at Greenway then", I said, "she's a beauty". "That's why Daddy's annoyed then, because the Lady Elizabeth' tender is missing and he wanted to greet them on the water and bring them ashore to Langham himself". "I know where the tender is, it's down at the FBI, or it was last night, I'll check on my way back and text you if it's still there, then your father can send someone down to bring it back". We said our goodbyes with a tender kiss and she was gone, and funnily, so had that empty feeling!

Chapter 7

The ride back downriver was a little choppy with an incoming tide and a fresh southerly breeze creating some spray. By the time I reached the FBI, I was quite wet and uncomfortable and was also a little surprised to see the tender still tied to the dock which meant Ricky had still not turned up. I tied alongside and stepped into the boat, found that the lifejackets were still strewn all over the place giving the impression that there had been either a struggle on board or Ricky had carried some very untidy passengers, who had just thrown the lifejackets into the boat when they docked. I don't know why, but I thought that a struggle was the most likely and used my smartphone to take a picture before putting them back where they belonged under the deck coaming. I started to replace them tidily when on one of the jackets I noticed there was what looked like a patch of blood, and stuck to it was Ricky's ticket for going too fast the day before. The blood was dry and the ticket was 'glued fast' to it and nearly tore as I separated the two. I put the bloodied lifejacket in my boat and the ticket in my pocket before rushing down the pontoon to the pub.

I startled the customers and the pub went eerily quiet when I opened the door with a crash, "is Ricky here"? I asked the barmaid; "not seen him" came the reply". Nobody had seen Ricky all weekend and despite me telling them that his boat had been tied up on the dock for the last twenty four hours, they were adamant that he had not been in the pub or been seen for a good few days. As I made my way back to the dock the ferry was pulling in, Terry, the captain who dropped me off at Sand Quay earlier was at the helm still, and as soon as the passengers disembarked I asked him if he'd seen Ricky, or anything suspicious. He said that he'd passed Ricky on the river the previous afternoon and that he had a passenger on board, a pretty young lady with short dark hair, but he thought nothing of it except that he was towing a small dinghy. He'd seen the tender tied to the Dittisham dock on his next trip and assumed they'd gone in the pub, although he didn't notice the dinghy. I was worried but did not say anything when I called Elizabeth. I told her the boat was safely tied up on the dock and they could pick it up but that Ricky was nowhere to be seen. I didn't mention the lifejackets or blood as not to worry her but decided to call DS Morgan. It was his day off and was clearly not keen to speak to me, but when I mentioned the blood he asked me to meet him at the Floating Bridge slipway in half an hour.

He was waiting when I arrived, wet for the second time from the spray and he helped me tie up. I showed him the bloodied lifejacket which he studied, and I told him I had some more information, "I'll keep this if you don't mind, I'll just pop it in the car and as I'm not officially on duty today, you can buy me a pint Bobby". We sat outside overlooking the higher ferry and although it was very busy, we found a table where we wouldn't be overheard. He listened to my story and was very interested in the picture I took. I also took out the speeding ticket from my pocket and gave it to him. I explained that the family were not overly concerned that Ricky was missing as it wasn't the first time he'd disappeared, but I felt there was more to it because I knew how important his big sister was to him, and that it was strange he hadn't even seen or called her since she'd arrived.

It was when I decided to tell him about Julie's nasty experience that his demeanour changed, he started shouting at me, and the whole dockside went quiet with everyone starring at us, even the people sat outside the pub and on the roof garden. He realised we were the focus of attention and calmed down but he was still really angry that I had not told him what had happened. I explained that Julie was understandably upset and frightened and that she had seen practically nothing because of the bag over her head. When I had seen her for coffee this morning, she told me she had woken up from a bad dream, and all she could remember was that the car was black or dark blue, like a small SUV, and that the man that dragged her into the car had dark hair. "Damn you Bobby, do you not realise that I'm on your side and that withholding information helps nobody other than the criminals". I apologised again and assured him that I would contact him immediately if anything else came up. He was happy with that and when I asked if he'd heard any news about the body yet, I was surprised that he was willing to share the information with me. I learnt, much to my surprise that it was a woman's body in her late-thirties, minus her hands, and despite extensive enquiries through the police records both locally and throughout the Cornwall and Devon Police area, there were no missing persons reported fitting her description. However, they had managed to obtain DNA and they were running it through the Police National Computer looking for a match. By the time we'd finished a second pint, which Bill Morgan had insisted on paying for, he had mellowed to the point of insisting I call him by his first name, 'Morgan', he loved a joke, "but not when I'm on duty though boyo", he'd quickly added. It was turning a little chilly, probably because my clothes were still a little damp so we shook hands and I went back to Pilgrim's tender and headed home.

    The dinner at Langham was an intimate yet formal affair in honour of the French Minister for Foreign and European affairs, Alain Dubois and his daughter Nicole. The family were gathering in the drawing room before making their way for drinks which had been organised aboard the minister's vessel, the Magie Noire for seven thirty. The telephone rang in the hall and George who was on his way to join the others answered, "yes sir, who may I say is calling", he listened for a moment, "could you just hold a moment and I will get him to the phone". George came into the room, "It's for you Uncle Ted, it's the Prime Minister's office". Ellen came in from the adjoining dining room, "everything is set for dinner, the room looks a picture with all those summer flowers from the garden and cook informs me that everything is under control in the kitchen". Ted came back into the drawing room smiling like a Cheshire cat, "I had hoped to let you know at dinner last night but now I can, the Prime Minister and her family are pleased to accept our invitation on Saturday for the Regatta Ball and will also stay until Sunday morning when they will leave for their summer holiday in Cornwall". A look of astonishment appeared on George and Elizabeth's face but Michael, Ellen and Grandpa had been given the 'heads up' when the invitation had been extended some little time before, and they were delighted. It would seem that the attendance of the French Minister had tipped the balance. "They expect to arrive late morning so that they may take in some of the Regatta's atmosphere in Dartmouth". "That is wonderful news Ted" said Ellen, "we'll get the master suite ready so that the children can be in the next room". It was indeed going to be an extra special event this year. Michael checked the time, "we must go, we don't want to keep the minister waiting do we"?

The Earl, Michael, Ellen and Sir Edward travelled the short distance to the dock in the Bentley whilst George and Elizabeth took the Range Rover. The tender which was styled on a classic Venetian water taxi, built in solid mahogany had been given a thorough clean, the wood polished to a mirror-like sheen and the blue striped seat cushions from the Lady Elizabeth had been arranged on the seats. They cruised the short distance down to Greenway in comfort and style, the journey taking a mere five minutes and were greeted aboard the Magie Noire by the minister. They were introduced to Nicole and the vessel's Captain and shown to the main saloon on the upper deck where every imaginable drink was available. George could not take his eyes off Nicole, who was dressed in a black evening dress with a single necklace of the most beautiful pearls. Formalities were forgotten for the evening with everyone addressed by their first names. Despite its stark and sinister outside appearance, the yacht was truly spectacular inside, very modern and light with every creature comfort imaginable. With accommodation for twelve in six cabins and a crew of seven you could understand why its illustrious owner preferred to stay on-board as opposed to staying even in the most luxurious of hotels. Following our tour, we settled in the main saloon with its drop-down balconies on both sides. George had now engaged Nicole in conversation and they seemed very relaxed in each other's company. Grandpa, Ted and Michael were talking politics and the problems the French were encountering with terrorist from North Africa who were increasingly targeting the French mainland, whilst Ellen and Elizabeth flitted between the two conversations adding their pennyworth. Ellen moved to one of the balconies to get a better view of an amazing sunset, which prompted everyone to take a look, and it turned out to be the cue that dinner would be ready at Langham. Thanks were extended to the crew and the party made their return to the tender for the short trip back upriver.

Dinner was an informal affair, the food chosen with emphasis on local produce, from the starter of locally sourced and smoked salmon, Devon beef from the South Devon herd on the estate and fresh strawberries from the farm orchards served with Devon clotted cream. The atmosphere was especially laid back the more the drinks flowed with Alain taking a surprising liking to Langham's red wine. The arrangements for the next day's visit to Plymouth were finalised with Alain confirming he would travel on the yacht, then spend a couple of days exploring Salcombe before returning in time for Saturday's big event. It was getting late, and with a big day ahead tomorrow, the guests expressed their sincere gratitude for a wonderful evening and insisted that it would be good if they stretched their legs and walk down to the dock. They were accompanied by Ted and George to the dock before they boarded the waiting Magie Noire's tender for their return to the yacht.

Chapter 8

Ricky opened his eyes but could see nor hear anything, it was pitch black and it was cold. He shivered and felt a single blanket over his otherwise naked body. He was lying on a very uncomfortable bed and it was pushed up against a bare wall, which he could feel had the shape and texture of cold stone. He had no idea where he was or how long he'd been there, and his recollection of what had happened was extremely hazy. He went to sit up but almost screamed in agony, it felt as if every bone in his body was broken. He sheepishly tried again to move and realised nothing was actually broken but he was badly bruised. He sat on the edge of the bed, wrapped the blanket around his body and tried to gather his thoughts as to what the hell was going on? His head felt heavy as if he'd had a bellyful of beer or maybe been drugged.

The mist started to clear from his muddled brain and he remembered heading home in the tender, he remembered passing the ferry rounding the bend in the river at Greenway. It was then that he spotted a girl in an inflatable dinghy, she'd lost an oar and was struggling to paddle the dinghy against the tide with one oar to retrieve it. Being a gentleman, and she being a very pretty young lady, he'd obviously gone to help. Pulling alongside, he remembered that alluring face with short black hair and an infectious smile. She was going back to her sailboat which was a short distance further upriver so he invited her aboard the tender and took the dinghy in tow, picking up the lost oar as they passed it. He remembered that her name was Nina and that she spoke perfect English but with foreign accent, which he thought had a hint of French in it. They had chatted about her trip along the coast from Weymouth and how she thought Dartmouth was a beautiful place.

They had arrived at her sailboat, and he'd been invited aboard for a quick drink. It was all flooding back to him now, he remembered Nina going down the companionway ladder and following, but there was someone else in the boat and he remembered his legs being grabbed from behind the ladder and tumbling head first into the saloon. He scrambled to his feet, Nina was headed for the V deck but the person who had grabbed his legs was approaching from behind the ladder, he remembered leaping for the hatchway missing several steps in his rush to escape, but his legs were grabbed again and he was being pulled back into the saloon; he grabbed the handles and using all his strength, kicked his legs and managed to free himself, stumbling into the cockpit. He thought he was free, but in his rush to get back into the tender he tripped on a rope and fell over the transom rail head first into the tender, crashing into the cubby and hitting his head senseless on the lifejacket locker, scattering them to all parts of the boat. He tried to get up but before he even turned over the man was over him and with a single blow to his jaw, the lights went out, until he had just woken.

Who were these people and what did they want with him? He suddenly remembered he was on his way to pick up his sister, Elizabeth; how long had he been unconscious; had he missed his sister's train? There were no answers forthcoming so he decided to check out his prison cell. He got up off the bed and despite the pain, he felt his way around the wall to the left of his bed, went along one complete wall of about four metres, round the corner and along another wall which was shorter, turned the corner again and immediately touched what felt like a wooden banister with steps rising. He was just about to feel his way up the steps when he heard a noise like a car starting and a dim light flickered above his head. Once his eyes adjusted to the light he could see that his prison was a dingy cellar in which the wooden bed and an old and dirty chemical toilet were the only items. The flagstone floor was cold and it seemed that the only way in and out was up the stairs to a stout wooden door.

He was on his way to investigate when he heard footsteps above heading for the door, two bolts were noisily slid open and the door opened. Two hooded men appeared at the top of the stairs and both started down the steps making Ricky tremble with fear. "Back on the bed" one of them called in a voice which clearly meant business. Ricky froze on the spot but they came towards him and before he could either move or gather his senses, he received a crushing blow to his solar plexus which knockout the wind out of him, sending a searing pain throughout his body which dropped him to his knees. Without stopping, the men grabbed his arms, one either side and manhandled him onto the bed. "If you do exactly as you are told, immediately and without question, no harm will come to you; disobedience will result in pain or even death. Do you understand"? Ricky was still trying to get his breath back and did not respond but the man who spoke violently struck him again, this time in the area of his right kidney which sent an even greater shocking pain throughout his body. "Do you understand"? The question was repeated. "Yes, yes, please don't hit me again" came a pathetic appealing reply. "Sit up now". He started to pull himself up but was too slow for his captors, but instead of administrating pain they again manhandled him up. The man nearest threw him a copy of The Times, "hold it in front of you" which Ricky complied with without hesitation, the man stepped back, took a phone out of his pocket, "look this way", and he took three or four photos, checked them and put the phone back. "Who are you, what do you want with me" chanced Ricky. "No questions" came the reply in a 'don't mess with me' voice. When one of the men went back up the stairs Ricky was desperate to ask how long they were planning on keeping him a prisoner but thought better of it. The man grabbed the newspaper back but Ricky was able to spot that it was Monday's paper which meant he had lost two days. The other man returned with a paper plate containing bread and cheese and a plastic bottle of water, and without further comment, they left the cellar, bolted the door and disappeared. A few moments later the light went out and Ricky noticed that the motor noise stopped. He guessed that it was a generator that provided the power for the light and assumed he was being held in a derelict building with no power, sanitation or running water. He suddenly realised how hungry he was and ate the food they'd left.

He was utterly confused as to why he was being held but assumed they had kidnapped him and were demanding a ransom from his family. Having lost two days meant that he could have been moved to almost anywhere but he made an assumption that staying fairly close to his home was less of a risk than traipsing across the country; and the man that spoke, he could not identify the accent. So many questions and no answers, he shivered again, took a gulp of the water and settled down on the bed under the inadequate blanket.

Sand Quay Marina had been a hive of activity since dawn, the Regatta 65 sailing yacht was being prepared for her sea trial whilst the Blue Dart 120 motor yacht was being steadily rolled out of the shed for her first taste of water. It is a proud moment for any yard when a boat is launched, but to have two on the same day was very special. I was on the Regatta's deck checking that all the systems were working and that all lines, fenders, boat hooks, lifejackets, flares and a myriad of other equipment was stowed away in their appropriate place. I would have two other crew members joining me for the trial, one of the yards engineers, Tom Stanley and the chief rigger, Brian Weston. We left the dock on the morning's ebbing tide with a gentle southerly wind, and headed under motor towards the mouth of the river.

With the start of the Regatta festivities only a couple of days away, the town was developing a carnival atmosphere with the bunting along both shores, flags from every imaginable seafaring nation fluttering in the breeze, and vessels of all descriptions criss-crossing the river. The town quay was awash with summer visitors, the ferries were packed and as we glided past the jetty, many an admiring glance was directed our way.

Once out of the river we turned east, hauled our sails and cut the motor. Passing the Mew Stone Rock, she gave a shudder and started to enjoy herself on a broad reach. The sailing heats for the Regatta were well under way with a colourful myriad of sails enjoying the morning breeze and stiff competition. This boat was the largest sailing vessel I had experienced at twenty metres or sixty five feet, but she could easily be sailed single handed. We tested all the electronic systems on-board including the radar, AIS and the chart plotter. Everything worked a dream and other than some minor adjustment of the standing rigging, we settled down to enjoy the experience. Past Old Mill Bay and the cove at Coleton Fishacre, which was once owned by the D'oyly Carte family who staged the Gilbert and Sullivan Savoy operas, but now owned by the National Trust, on past the old Coastguard Cottage at Scabbacombe Sands where a small sloop was anchored with its dinghy pulled up onto the beach, St. Mary's Bay and eventually rounding Berry Head into Torbay. Trawlers from Brixham were out in force as were the seagulls that swarm above the boats fighting over scraps thrown overboard. With valuable catches of scallop, sole and crab amongst a large variety of fish caught locally, the port was thriving. It was Torbay Regatta week and the bay was stunning in the early afternoon sun with hundreds of small sailing boats enjoying a perfect day on the water.

We had put the boat through an array of checks and had tacked, gybed and tested each point of sail on our outward journey. The return to Dartmouth would be a much more relaxed affair and we settled down to enjoy a near perfect sea trial. I had brought my binoculars from Pilgrim and was watching a group of walkers on the SW Coast path above Scabbacombe Cottage. I moved the binoculars down onto the little sailboat anchored. Close up, she looked a bit of an old dog but she must have been loved at one time for she was called 'Poppet', and she hailed from Weymouth. There was a young lady in the cockpit, the dinghy was tied off the aft cleat and she was preparing to get underway.

I heard my phone ring in the saloon and Tom's face appeared at the top of the companionway ladder clutching it. I answered and was surprised to hear Elizabeth's voice. She was distraught, sobbing like a child, "whatever is the matter"? I asked. "It's Ricky, he's been kidnapped" she wailed, "we thought he'd been on another drinking binge but he's been kidnapped and they're demanding five million pounds if we want to see him alive again". She was talking so fast, mumbling and sobbing all at the same time. "Slow down" I said, "who's taken him"? I don't know, Daddy's had an email at work with a picture of Ricky, he looks awful so Daddy says and they're demanding five million by Friday". She was slowly pulling herself together, "Mummy is beside herself and Daddy and George are still with the French Minister, I know you and Ricky were friends Bobby, can you come over"? She was babbling again and I could hear Ellen crying in the background." I'm sorry Elizabeth, I'm out on the boat and won't get back to the marina for another couple of hours; have you called the police". "Oh no Bobby, Daddy says the email has warned him not to involve the police otherwise Ricky will be fish food". She burst out crying again, "please don't tell anyone Bobby, I beg you". "I promise Elizabeth, but I really do think your father should contact DS Morgan at the very least". "No Bobby, no no no, we are not going to risk Ricky's life, and I would be really angry with you if you do such a thing," and with that, she hung up.

"Everything alright Bobby"? asked Tom. "Everything's fine Tom, how are you getting on down below"? "Almost done, just a few more checks and I'm finished". The sail back to Sand Quay was uneventful and we docked next to the Blue Dart 120, which now stood proud on the outer pontoon. A couple of the marina hands had been tasked with washing the boat down and as I stepped onto the dock I spotted my father on the motor yachts' upper deck. I hadn't had a good look at the new model and walked up the gangplank into a world of luxurious opulence. She was indeed the yards' flagship, the interior crafted in the best English oak with calf leather upholstery and polished chrome fittings. Father and Tim were inspecting the final snag list from this morning's survey and waved me over. They wanted to know how the trial had gone and were really pleased with my comments.

I debated telling them about Ricky and thought I should. My father was shocked and kept asking if I was sure that he hadn't just done a bunk. I think my father had a bit of a low opinion of Ricky through his reputation as a bit of a womaniser, and I was a bit shocked when he intimated that the family should not pay a penny to kidnappers. I did suggest that I hoped he would view the circumstances a little differently if I had been kidnapped, to which I thought I detected a slight nod of his head, which was not overly convincing.

Tim took me on the grand tour and I was overwhelmed with the quality of design and materials which surpassed other yachts from mainstream manufacturers I had seen at various boat shows. I sat at the helm on the bridge for some considerable time as much to admire the array of electronics on-board as to contemplate Ricky's situation. I called DS Morgan's number but it went through to his voicemail; I chickened out!

Chapter 9

The train to London was thundering through the countryside, packed with commuters, students and families heading for a day out in the city. On board was DS Morgan heading for Scotland Yard no less, a place he'd read about but had never graced its hallowed corridors. There had been developments, the DNA result had been run through the Police National Computer in Hendon which had revealed a name and an address for the dead woman, and DS Morgan was on his way to try and find a motive and a lead as to who might have committed the crime on his patch.

His first port of call was a meeting with the Serious Crime Command officers who had been assigned the case. The view from the eighteenth floor was spectacular and he could see the Thames downriver as far as Tower Bridge and St. Paul's. Coffee and biscuits were a life saver after four hours on a packed train and he indulged without shame. A young Detective Constable had prepared a presentation of the information they had gathered and she first put up a picture of the dead woman taken ten years before. The DNA had revealed a Hannah Parker, aged twenty nine at the time of her arrest which would make her forty now if she were still alive, who had been arrested then for a minor drug offence. It was her only record and it really was minor, the possession of cannabis. It was a lucky break, as without that single 'crime' she would have otherwise remained unidentified. It also revealed her occupation as a housekeeper at the Grosvenor Hotel just around the corner from 'The Yard'. The address on the record was in South London at Clapham which would be their first port of call.

The address was a tidy tree lined street of two storey Victorian houses, most of which had been converted into two flats. The names on the two bell pushes were no clue but they pressed the ground floor intercom and an elderly lady's voice answered. The lady Detective constable assigned to him for the day introduced herself and the door clicked open. She was a sweet old lady who insisted on making them a cup of tea. She had known Hannah for the past four years before she had moved away four months earlier, and said that she was very neighbourly. She hadn't seen much of her because she seemed to work very long hours and didn't seem to have any friends or visitors who visited her at home, but she did know that she regularly visited her mum in Devon who was not very well, and she had hoped to find a job more local so that she could look after her. Bingo! There was a local connection and he was confident that this new information would open more doors. They spent another half hour with the old lady, but there was no more useful information forthcoming. They thanked her and made their way to the door and called the first floor intercom. A young woman came down the stairs carrying a small baby. It was soon clear that she had never met Hannah as they had moved in after Hannah had left. They again thanked her for her time and headed back towards Victoria.

Next stop was the Grosvenor Hotel's Human Resources Department where a very helpful young man took out Hannah's file. She had worked with them for four years and were sorry to see her leave. She had been utterly reliable and conscientious, a rarity in this business, he had expressed. He checked the file for any mention of a job offer or a request for a reference but there were none, and he was not aware of any particular close friend at the hotel. It seemed that most housekeeping vacancies were filled from specialist agencies but there were none on Hannah's file. They had now hit a brick wall and it was unlikely that his visit to London would reveal any further clues.

Once they were back at Scotland Yard, DS Morgan called Dartmouth to update the local officers and get them to search for the address of all the

'Parker's' in the area, although they had Hannah's date of birth which should narrow down the search, and with that, he thanked his fellow officers and headed back to Paddington for his train home.

The tour and meetings at the plant in Plymouth had been a tremendous success and unbeknown to the minister, they had launched one of the Skylark drones over the city prior to his arrival. When they entered the control room, a replay of the 'Magie Noire's arrival at the marina was on the large screen with an equally large screen showing a live close-up of the vessel with the crew washing down her decks, but what delighted and somewhat frightened the minister was another replay on a third screen of Nicole walking on Plymouth Hoe with the image so clear that not only could they see her white rose neck tattoo, but the word 'Monique' under it, and all from18,000 feet. The orders for four Skykite and four Skylark drones were already placed by the French Defence Ministry and following today's visit, would be rubber stamped within the government. The French Minister had long since left to re-join his yacht which had docked at the Queen Anne's Battery Marina in the Barbican area of the city. Michael,

Michael, George and Ted had continued their discussions, but were more focused on Ricky's kidnapping and the outrageous ransom demand. They had come to the conclusion that it was more likely that it was politically motivated, and that a terrorist cell operating in the UK was responsible. The only lead they had was the email address which didn't give away much as it was a common 'yahoo.com' email and Ted guessed that although it may have originated in the UK it was almost certain that it would have been sent via a Virtual Private Network using multiple proxy servers all over the world which would be virtually impossible to trace. Ted had however through his many experts at the Foreign Office forwarded the message to them and they in turn were in contact with GCHQ. Although they had not involved the local police, they had contacted the Counter Terrorism Command at the Metropolitan Police who had been sceptical that it was nothing more than an attempt to extort money from a wealthy family. They had advised him to contact the local Devon and Cornwall force who would have officers experienced in kidnapping. Michael read the email again, it was short and not very specific, it read;

"To Sir Michael Gilbert, your son, Richard Gilbert has been abducted and is held for a ransom of five million pounds sterling to be paid within four days. Payment instructions will be given in a later email. No negotiations will be undertaken and failure to fully comply will result in his torture and death. Any police involvement will result in his immediate execution".

Maybe they were right, the spelling and grammar was too perfect for a foreign terrorist group and that some thugs were looking to make a quick killing! He had called Ellen several times and although she was being comforted by Elizabeth, she remained distraught. Grandpa was also on his way home and although Michael felt he should also be there, he had no clue what else he could do. He had already spoken to the bank and they were already in the process of transferring the money into his personal account. He decided to be bold, and replied to the kidnappers that he did not negotiate either, and that unless they released his son unharmed, he would bring down the full force of the law on their heads. He read his reply again, considered the possible consequences and pressed the send button. He was shocked by his own actions but convinced himself that he was right not to roll over in the face of such pressure, then felt guilty and worried at the same time that it would put Ricky at some considerable risk. Could he live with the potential consequences and the undoubted wrath of his family? He went home to comfort his wife and await the next move from his sons' captors.

Out in the estate's apple orchard, the pickers were hard at work harvesting the early crop Devon Crimson cider apples. The old Fordson Major tractor with its hopper attached was almost full with the ripe apples and Mo was getting ready to take them back and unload into one of the two cider presses at the Cider Works and Museum at Langham. On this particular day, it was particularly busy with families and coachloads of pensioners enjoying the tour and especially the ploughman's lunches which accompanied the Cider. He was known simply as Mo but his real name was Mohamed Beghal, a French Algerian terrorist convicted of plotting to bomb the Strasbourg Cathedral, but managed to escape from a Paris prison and was on Interpol's most wanted list. He had arrived with a group of European fruit pickers to work the orchards a month earlier and had waited for such a busy day so that his fellow workers would be distracted long enough for him to remove one of the many empty cider barrels into his hopper. He took the tractor around the back of the Cider Works, took a quick look around, and within a few seconds, the barrel was safely secured in the hopper. Instead of driving straight back to where the pickers were, he drove amongst the lines of apple trees down to the bottom edge of the orchard, stopped and hid the barrel in a bush close to the river where he could easily retrieve it after work. He was back with the pickers before he was missed.

Nina had turned 'Poppet' into the Dart and was sailing in on the flow tide. The late afternoon sun was casting long shadows across the river with most of Dartmouth in the shade whilst Kingswear on the eastern bank was bathed in sunshine. The rowing heats for the Regatta were still in full swing and there was a sight that intrigued her taking place adjacent the sailing club; four men in a rowing boat were pulling against what appeared to be a bungee attached to one of the sailing club pilings, with two men in a small dinghy apparently measuring how far they could row before the bungee hauled them back. She would never understand these mad English and their cricket and rugby and now a new sport to her, bungee rowing. She did have to admit that they appeared to be having a whale of a time with raucous laughter and howling from what sounded like inebriated heathens. Nina was a strict Muslim whose real name was Yasmine Wadoud, a leading light of the Algerian Islamic militant group, Al-Qaeda in the Islamic Maghreb. She was also one of the terrorist cell operating in the UK. Poppet sailed past Greenway, around the big bend at Dittisham and on towards the Harbourne River, a tributary of the Dart. She aimed the boat close to Kirkham Copse and dropped the anchor close to the bank in an area of the river which was fairly isolated other than the passing river traffic. It also happened to be on the edge of the Langham orchard, and she didn't have to wait for long before she heard Mohammed's footsteps approaching through the copse. She pulled the dinghy close, checked the river traffic which was clear, rowed the ten feet to the bank and took the empty barrel and her passenger on board. They were back on the boat in less than five minutes and Mohammed went down into the saloon and stayed out of sight for the return sail downriver and back to the cove at Scabbacombe Cottage.

The two brand new yachts at Sand Quay were glistening in the low setting sun, the crew and I with some of the young lads from the yard headed for Smugglers for a snack. As soon as I smelled food, I realised we had missed lunch so it was not surprising that I was ravenous. Smugglers was based on an American style waterfront diner with good wholesome fried and grilled meats and fish served generally with fries or jacket potatoes. The brainchild of a chef who had one too many holidays in Florida, it attracted a diverse clientele who enjoyed its beachy style which could be accessed by road or on the water. I settled down with a blackened, grilled grouper with fries, coleslaw and salad, a cold beer and good company. I would have enjoyed it even more if I could just get Ricky out of my mind. Earlier, I had called Elizabeth who was trying to console an extremely upset and worried mother. We talked for a long while but I decided that there was nothing to be gained by going over to Langham. It was very much a family affair but I couldn't help thinking that I could do something to help. Whatever had happened to Ricky, it had happened on the river and there was nobody who knew the river better than

I did. I ate my caramel cheesecake, supped the last of my beer and headed down to the dock.

Pilgrim's tender was just inviting me to take a trip to see if I could find any clues as to where he may be. I pushed off the dock, fired the outboard and meandered out into the river. I intended to check out any buildings, occupied, empty or derelict along both banks of the river and the creeks and tributaries leading off it all the way up to Totnes if necessary. I checked out old boathouses and abandoned mills, derelict tanneries, ordinary, if expensive family homes and the homes of the privileged. I checked in the hedgerows, under bridges and industrial sheds on the upper river and along the Baltic Wharf and Steamer Quay in Totnes, but the only significant incident was shortly after I passed the Galmpton inlet where a small sailboat helmed by a young lady with short dark hair and pulling a dinghy passed going down the river. She was called Poppet, and I had seen her before!

It was dark by the time the train pulled in to Totnes station, DS Morgan was pleased with the day's work, especially as a phone call from his colleagues in Dartmouth had revealed an address in Paignton for the Parkers'. It would appear that Hannah's father had died some five years ago in an accident on one of Brixham's trawlers but her mother was still alive. He looked at his watch and decided that it was too late to pay a visit tonight, besides he was exhausted; it would wait until the morning.

Ricky was pacing up and down his dark cold cellar trying to keep warm. He was hungry and hurting, he felt dirty but most of all he was cold. It was the middle of summer, yet this cellar was damp and cold which was probably made worse by lack of food. He heard a car pull up, the first sound he'd heard for hours but he was both glad that he might be fed, but also trembling with the fear of being hurt again. He heard footsteps above, just one person as far as he could tell, then the light flickered with the sound of the generator which gave him some comfort. But nobody came. It seemed an eternity before he heard a door open, more footsteps and faint voices, he couldn't make out whether it was two people or more. He contemplated calling or banging on the door but decided it was not a good idea, and sat back down on the bed. It wasn't long before the bolts were drawn and two figures appeared at the top of the stairs. They were still hooded, but as they approached he instantly recoiled on the bed as he could tell from their aggression that something was wrong. "Sit on the side of the bed" came the command, and Ricky must have been slow to react because he was manhandled onto the edge of the bed. "We can do this the easy painless way or the difficult painful way, sit still", and with that he pulled out a cordless hair trimmer, the noise of which startled

Ricky and made him jump. "Why are you shaving my head"? he asked as clumps of his boyish, golden locks fell to the floor. "Sit still and be quiet if you want to eat tonight" and with that, he did as they demanded with a tear in his eye, not because of his hair, but because of the seemingly helpless situation he was in. They kicked the pile of hair aside with their feet, stepped back and again took the phone out to take a picture. With that the second man went back up the stairs and reappeared with the same plate of bread, cheese and a bottle of water. They went to leave and Ricky couldn't help himself but had ask why and how long they were going to keep him locked up. The man nearest turned in a threatening way making Ricky spill his bread and cheese on to the hair covered floor, they laughed and both went up the stairs throwing the bolts as they left. All Ricky kept thinking was that he was going to be even colder without his hair, and when he retrieved his hair covered food, he could have cried, but he still had some inner strength, brushed the hairs away and ate.

Chapter 10

Michael awoke early as he always did on days he needed to go into his office, but this morning he had decided to work from home. Ellen was still angry with him for sending the email reply that he had to the kidnappers, which would endanger Ricky's life, but he had argued that rolling over could also make matters worse, especially that there was no guarantee that he would be released even if the ransom was paid. He switched on the computer in his office to pick up his emails knowing there would be a reaction to his reply, and there it was, the image shocked him, Ricky was bald with a nasty gash on his forehead where his hairline used to be. His eyes seemed bigger and redder than he'd ever noticed and the message was curt and to the point:

"To Sir Michael Gilbert, do not mess with us, the next body parts we remove will involve blood and suffering. Have the money ready by Friday and we will send instructions on how to transfer".

Ted was up, he'd heard him in the breakfast room and although he wasn't hungry, he joined him for coffee. Ted also thought he had been too rash in his reply, and felt he should have at least waited until there was news from his Foreign Office staff. He told Ted about the picture and handed him a copy of the email which he had printed. "It looks as if they've shaved his head and knocked him about a bit, might even knock a bit of sense into him", a comment he quickly regretted because Ellen was stood behind him. "How could you be so cruel Michael, Ricky's life is in real danger and all you can do is make flippant comments when you should be securing his freedom". "Hang on a minute Ellen, what I should have done is gone to the police straight away so that they can catch these criminals and not fund their life of crime". "This is Ricky's life you're talking about, our Ricky" she was sobbing again "and all you can think about is not losing five million pounds", and with that she left the room and slammed the door. "You don't know how lucky you are Ted, women get so emotional about everything". Ted was astonished, "you don't know how lucky you are Michael, if a wife can't get emotional about the life of her kidnapped son, then she's not a good mother". Michael realised he'd been insensitive and headed after her. "See if your contacts have come up with anything please Ted, we're running out of time here" and disappeared out of the door.

Ellen was in the Orangery, pottering around with plants as she always did when she wanted to be alone. "I'm sorry Ellen, I'm just as concerned as you are and want to see that boy of ours back home, but I also want to ensure that they don't hold all the aces. It would be easy to just pay up, but that alone won't guarantee his safe return". Ellen was looking at Ricky's picture and reading the email copy I'd given her. "I know you'll do everything to get him back but we don't know how far these people will go, and we'll probably only get one chance to ensure his safe release". "I've already transferred the money into our private account and Ted is doing everything at his end. We have until Friday, so try not to worry". He gave her a loving hug and headed back to his office to consider the advice from the Counter Terrorism people in London. He picked up the phone and dialled the number of Devon and Cornwall Police Headquarters in Exeter.

Back in Dartmouth, DS Morgan had picked up the information he needed and he and a WPC were on their way to Paignton to find Hannah's mother. The address turned out to be a small bungalow in Preston and they parked and rang the doorbell. There was no reply, he lifted the letter box to see if there was any sign of life and saw a pile of accumulated mail on the carpet inside the door. They peered in through a window which was a small bedroom, went around to the back revealing a small conservatory and lounge next to which there was a small kitchen. It didn't look as if the kitchen had been used for some time but as they were about to leave an old gentleman's head appeared above the fence; "you're trespassing, go away before I call the police" he said. He was better than a Rottweiler but calmed down when DS Morgan said "we are the police" and showed him his badge. He calmed down and told them that Evelyn Parker had a stroke and was in the Roundhouse Nursing Home in Paignton. When asked about Hannah, he expressed surprise that she hadn't been around for a long time, "she used to visit her mum at least every couple of weeks and stay in the bungalow, but we haven't seen her", he said.

They sat back in the car, "well, all is not lost, we've got another shot at solving this mystery. The Roundhouse Nursing Home please driver", he said and within a short while they were parking in the visitor's bay. A lovely lady on reception confirmed that Evelyn Parker was a resident but also warned them that she'd suffered a severe stroke and was unable to talk or do anything for herself. She took them through to her room and Morgan realised they were up a cul de sac, not only was she unable to speak, she was not even aware of their presence in the room. There were family pictures on the locker beside her bed, and one picture which caught Morgan's eye of Hannah looked fairly recent. He enquired whether she received any letters from Hannah, but there were no letters from anybody. He asked if he could borrow the picture and the receptionist doubted if Evelyn would miss it.

They headed back to Dartmouth to make further enquiries. There had to be someone who new Hannah and her whereabouts between leaving The Grosvenor Hotel and finding a job nearer her mum. He opened up two lines of enquiry, he called his contact at the Met. and requested her to return to the Grosvenor to interview some of the housekeeping staff who knew her, and may have used the same employment agency to find new work. He also had WPC Thompson phone all the major hotels within a five mile radius to check if they had received a job application or made a job offer to a Hannah Parker.

Julie was at her desk when I climbed the stairs from her father's shop. "Hi Bobby, I thought that was your voice I heard downstairs, what brings you slumming it over on this side of the river"? "I came for your help, but first you have to make me a solemn promise that what I'm about to tell you goes no further, for the time being at least". "Of course Bobby, what is it"? "No Julie, I mean it, no publication behind my back, no telling anyone, family or friend". That got her attention and she turned her chair to face me. "OK Bobby, I promise, now what is it you want to tell me"? I told her Ricky's story right down to the ransom note and my suspicions, and I also told her that DS Morgan was aware of her own kidnapping. She sat there agog about Ricky and was not at all annoyed that I had told Morgan about her adventure. She asked a myriad of questions and I could see she was already framing a story. I answered all her questions and reminded her again that any leaking of this new now would put Ricky's life in danger, and Julie herself.

"Now, let's see if you're of any use to me in trying to find out what the hell it's going on here. Are you able to access boat registration information, specifically who owns Poppet"? She had never tried to get information on a boat but she confided that a press pass was good at opening doors. I told her I needed to know who owns Scabbacombe Cottage and specifically, who handles the bookings and who is currently renting? "That's easy Bobby, I can find that out inside an hour". "But you have to be careful Julie, I don't want these people to know that someone is making enquiries about them, besides, if they are who I suspect, they are dangerous, they are probably the people that gave you that car ride so don't go in there like the cavalry". "What do you plan to do with the information, are you going to the police with it"? "I'd like to take a closer look myself first", I said, "and I'm sure that 'Poppet' is the key, I think it was used to kidnap Ricky in the first place and I wouldn't be surprised if he was still being held on-board, so I'm planning to take a little 'looksee' tonight". "I'll come with you". "No you bloody won't, it's far too dangerous and besides if something happens to me you can go to Morgan with everything you know". Julie had to admit that it made sense so she didn't argue any more. "Call me when you've got some information", and with that I got up to leave. "Where are you going now" she asked, I'm taking Pilgrim out for a jolly so that I can take a closer look without risking any suspicion". "You be careful, I don't want my story ruined by an amateur" she said with a smirk on her face. "So it's your story already", I laughed, gave her a peck on the cheek and left.

Sand Quay was even busier with more and more boats arriving every day with the start of the Regatta only two days away. Pilgrim was ready to go, and I headed downriver against the tide under motor, but as soon as I turned East at the bar, I raised the sails and headed towards Torbay. As I drew closer to Scabbacombe Cottage, there was no 'Poppet' in sight, damn I thought, but at least I could take a closer look at the cottage. The old Coastguard cottage was nestled against the hill in an unparalleled position with unrestricted views of the sea, and with the South West Coast Path meandering along the cliffs behind it. I slowed my passage and took out the powerful binoculars that were always on Pilgrim. The cottage looked deserted, no cars were parked and there were no people in close proximity. I spotted some walkers about half a mile away on the path heading towards Coleton Fishacre, but no other signs of life. I didn't turn her bow back to the West for at least half an hour just in case someone was keeping a lookout. I turned Pilgrim into the wind and tacked for a heading back to Dartmouth. I slowed her progress again as Scabbacombe came into view searching every nook and cranny around the cottage for signs of life, but there was none.

Heading back towards the Mew Stone Rock and the estuary I caught a glimpse of 'Poppet' edging her nose out of the river, I immediately changed course for more open water and headed out towards the Start Point Light to avoid passing too close and raising any suspicion. I expected 'Poppet' to turn eastwards towards the cottage but she seemed to be heading straight out to sea. I kept my course to put some distance between us and was careful not to use the binoculars until it was obvious that we were on a different heading. Pilgrim was a fully equipped vessel with the latest in electronic navigation and a powerful radar. I turned on the radar and overlaid it on the chart plotter to see how strong an echo 'Poppet' was returning and to get a fix and bearing so that I could shadow her at a safe distance. Her echo was very weak which meant that I would have to keep a visual sight of her during the remainder of daylight hours but could move in closer at dusk and use the radar. She was on a bearing of 143 degrees, or SSE which if she kept that course would take her to Guernsey. I continued away from her towards

Start Point and when I was four miles out, turned Pilgrim onto a parallel course and settled down in the cockpit for what could be a long night.

My phone rang, it was Julie, "where are you" she said, "heading for Guernsey at the moment shadowing Poppet, and I still don't know whether I'm on a wild goose chase or not". "Can't help you there" she said, "but I have some news for you, the cottage is owned by a local family and has done for the last thirty years, they only let it through one agency and although they were reluctant to give me the name of the current renter, I used my charm and have the name of a French couple who've rented it for the whole month of August, a Mr and Mrs N Laurent with an address in Marseille". "Doesn't give us much does it, could be genuine I suppose, and what about the boat"? "Well there is a connection, and this will cost you an expensive dinner because I had to buy the full history from the boat registry people, she was purchased in May and registered by the broker to a Mrs Nina Laurent at the same address in Marseille". "So we have a definite connection between the cottage and boat but nothing out of the ordinary or remotely suspicious. I may well be chasing shadows out here too but I'll stay with it and see where it leads. I'll give you a call when I'm back in the Dart". "Take care, speak to you later", and with that I concentrated on keeping Poppet in sight.

She sailed the same course other than a brief period to cross the shipping lanes and for the last hour I had moved Pilgrim to within two miles and was tracking her weak signal with the radar. It was now dark and as far as I could see she was not using her navigation lights, and I was forced to follow suit. A half hour later, the radar picked up a stronger echo from a much larger vessel that appeared to be converging on Poppet and within the next few minutes, the two echoes merged and stopped moving. Although I could see nothing, I assumed that the two vessels had pulled alongside each other and some sort of transfer was taking place. Within five minutes, the echoes parted again and I could tell that Poppet was now heading back on a bearing of 323 degrees, NNW towards the cottage. I turned Pilgrim around put up every available sail and headed back satisfied that there was no more to be gained by shadowing her back.

An hour out of Dartmouth, the Northern horizon lit up in a blaze of light with a spectacular fireworks display. This was Torbay Regatta's fireworks night with one of the best exhibition of pyrotechnics on the South Coast. It was all over in fifteen minutes and it was as if heaven had been disturbed, for it started to rain, a gentle drizzle at first followed by a thunderous downpour with forked lightning to the East, as if God himself was competing for the best show of the night. It was the first drop of rain for weeks and it was very welcome as long as it didn't last long enough to spoil the Garden Party and the rest of the week's Regatta events.

I was back in the Dart by ten thirty just in time to meet Julie for a swift drink in the Castle. The bar was busy and Julie was in a really jolly mood. She was dressed in a white blouse and tight fitting jeans and I wondered why I hadn't noticed how beautiful she was before. We seemed utterly relaxed in each other's company, talking about schooldays and the people we knew and laughing out loud when we recalled some hilarious moments. I don't know whether it was a rush of blood or whether she'd done another good job on me, but before we left, I had invited her to be my guest at the Regatta Ball and she had jumped for joy, put her arms around my neck and given me the most passionate kiss I could ever remember. For some reason, parting was more difficult tonight, and I couldn't help looking back over my shoulder as I walked back to the boat with a skip to my step.

Nina had also successfully navigated Poppet back to Scabbacombe and safely anchored her in the cove. She had transported her precious cargo in the dinghy and delivered it safely to Karin, the third member of the cell to use his specialist skills.

Chapter 11

Hawley had been hive of activity from the early morning in readiness for this afternoon's Garden Party. Workmen had already put up some pretty green and white striped marquee's and ornamental lighting the previous evening and a line of vans were descending with everything from posh white cane tables and chairs, small staging for the band, table linen, beers, wines and spirits, and everything else imaginable to make this one of the social events on the Dartmouth calendar. There were two hog roasts already cooking and two more ready to light in a little while. The caterers were busy preparing freshly picked produce for a typical English summer party. The overnight rain had cleared leaving a fresh sunny morning, the sun's rays beginning to warm the garden. The auctioneers were preparing the lots for the charity auction, art including sculptures and paintings, many by local artists, and all manner of highly prized goods and artefacts would be up for grabs to the highest bidder with all the proceeds going to local charities.

Mother was busy getting the house ready for Brother Nathan and his family and she was even more excited at seeing Pippa again. The excitement didn't even stop there because Tim's new young lady, Georgina would also be there and she couldn't help herself from walking around singing and with a silly grin on her face.

The men were otherwise engaged, Robert and Tim were down at the marina preparing the Blue Dart 120 for its short move onto the town moorings ready for their invited guests and prospective customers to be entertained during the Regatta events. I had already left the pontoon in the Regatta 65 with the crew that would man the sailing flagship for the duration of the event. We were on the river watching HMS Somerset, a Royal Navy Frigate manoeuvre into her position between two large buoys in the centre of the river. She had returned from anti-piracy and counter terrorism duties East of Suez in the Gulf and Indian Ocean via Gibraltar, and her crew would enhance Dartmouth's association with the Royal Navy through ceremonial duties and by entering several crews for both the sailing and rowing events. When she was safely moored, we were able to take up one of our two fixed moorings a little upriver. With a powerful engine and bow thrusters we had secured her in no time and I was able to catch one of the many water taxis that plied the river back to Sand Quay.

Ricky's world was still in darkness although he could still hear the generator running close by. He had heard a car start its engine earlier and was expecting his prison cell to descend into lonely silence as was the norm, but he could hear muted voices, one he believed was a woman's voice and occasional metallic tapping coming from above. He also had the occasional whiff of a sweet sickly smell that was familiar but he could not quite make out. He had lain on his bed for the past hour contemplating how he could escape. There was only one opportunity each day when they brought him his bread and cheese and he had determined that he would attempt a surprise for them and get himself out of his predicament, because he was now sure that no help was forthcoming from the outside world.

Michael was in his office at Langham with Ted, who had heard back from his contacts at the Foreign Office but the news was not what he'd hoped. As feared, the original emails would likely be sent from the UK to a contact in North Africa, probably Algeria using VPN and bounced around multiple servers in a dozen countries and then forwarded back to the UK; the same in reverse for the replies which were virtually untraceable. Officers from Devon and Cornwall police had met with him yesterday evening and had taken a recent photo of Ricky. They had also spent time checking through the personnel files of Estate workers because they said that most of these types of crime were perpetrated by people known to the family, either a family member, which he had told them was preposterous, friends or employees. Their plan was to check the names against known criminals, and after a whole two hours had left. Michael was not sure he had done the right thing, and as they discussed it, his email box pinged with a new message. It read:

"To Sir Michael Gilbert, we expressly instructed you not to contact the police and you have ignored our demands. As a result, your son will bear the punishment for your actions and the price of his release is increased to six million pounds. Payment will be made as follows: You are to open a Bitcoin online account and exchange your six million pounds for the equivalent number of bitcoins (today's exchange is equivalent of 11,538 bitcoins) and transfer the exact amount to an address which will be as advised. You are warned that this transaction must be completed by midnight Friday. No further warnings will be issued".

"What the hell are Bitcoins"? yelled Michael, "where will these bastards stop, six fucking million Ted, why do they assume we have that sort of money? How the hell do they know that the police have been here, they must be watching the house or one of those bastards is working here on the estate"? "Michael, I wouldn't normally allow anyone to pay a ransom, but when it happens to your own family, how can I advise you against", said Ted, "do what they say, get ready to do the transaction and hope that the police turn something up before Friday night". Ted explained that bitcoins were a relatively new unregulated internet currency used widely by criminals to launder money, buy arms and drugs but also had an increasing commercial use for all types of goods. The exchange was very volatile but its advantage was that both sender and receiver remained totally anonymous. "I don't like it Ted, I'm not in control of this one am I"? Ted could give him no comfort, they were both helpless and hoped that some divine intervention might prevail.

When Ted had left, Michael closed the door and dialled the number of a Private Investigator he had once used in Plymouth. He spoke quietly in case there was indeed a spy in the household!

DS Morgan was not getting anywhere either, all their enquiries had kicked up were three job applications by Hannah Parker, one at the Grand Hotel, Torquay, one at the TLH Leisure Resort also in Torquay and one locally at the Dart Marina Hotel and Spa, all three rejected with the reason given as 'no vacancies'. They were still checking London and Local hospitality agencies but nothing there either. He picked up the phone, dialled a number and it rang; it was answered, "Bobby, why is it I have to find out about local crimes from other people when I am one hundred percent certain that you knew before me, and despite our conversation a few days ago, you chose not to share it with me"? I knew straight away what he was getting at, and he caught me totally flat footed. "DS Morgan, it's good to hear from you too, what crime are we talking about"? "You must think that we police officers cannot be trusted with sensitive information that affects a person's life, yet when you're in trouble yourself, you deem it OK to call upon our help. I am of course talking about Ricky". He was pissed off with me, probably justified, but I decided to act dumb. "I told you about my concerns about Ricky's disappearance on Sunday evening". He cut me off, "don't piss me off lad, you know that it is now an official kidnap investigation with a ransom demand and the threat of death. At what point did you consider this might turn serious"? "I'm sorry you feel that I've withheld information from you DS Morgan, but the truth is that I received a phone call from a distraught Lady Elizabeth on Monday afternoon and I advised her to contact the police, but because of the warning contained in the ransom, she begged me not to tell anyone and I promised I would not". "Now why do I think that you would not have left it at that, do you have something I should know about that would help get Ricky back safely". "I don't at this time Sir". "Bobby, I'm disappointed with you, I thought we had an understanding, but obviously not, but if I find out you're lying to me Bobby, then you will have a serious problem". With that, he hung up and I felt decidedly uncomfortable.

"Who was that Bobby, are you OK"? I turned, it was Grandma, she was always alert and could detect a lie just from the tone of one's voice. "Nothing Grandma, just DS Morgan filling me in on the body I found". She gave me one of those unbelieving looks but said no more and carried on talking with the auctioneer.

The garden looked a picture, everything was organised with military precision and the smell of those hog's cooking was really making me hungry. I could hear loud voices in the house, recognised Uncle Nathan's booming tones and mother laughing at something he'd said. Family was arriving, I checked my watch as I had been detailed to pick up Pippa from the station. I headed inside to say hello to the family, the hall was awash with bodies and luggage, Uncle Nathan was bigger than ever with a right portly and ample stomach hanging grotesquely over his belt, and it looked as if Oliver, his son was going the same way. I liked Uncle Nathan, he really was a jolly chap with the loudest, boomiest voice I'd ever heard, cousin Oliver was sullen on the other hand, seemed to lack interest in anything with the exception of food, drink and banking, which he had followed his father into, and by all accounts was doing rather well at it. Amanda on the other hand had blossomed into an attractive eighteen year old and although shy, had bloomed in every department since I had last seen her. Margaret, the long suffering wife and mother was her usual self, quiet, preferring to stay in the background, although at one family gathering, someone had plied her with drink and she became hilariously funny especially during a game of charades. Uncle Nathan embraced me with such enthusiasm I could not breathe, "how are you my boy, that brother of mine not working you too hard it's he"? "No Uncle, I'm a very fortunate chap". "Make the most of it lad, it'll all change when you take a wife, which reminds me, we've been expecting an invitation to your wedding far too long, how is the Lady Elizabeth". "Long story Uncle, I remain a confirmed bachelor for the foreseeable future at least. Will you excuse me, I must go and change, I'm to pick up Pippa shortly from the station", and with that I bounded up the stairs.

By the time I left, Jazzmatazz, a six piece authentic New Orleans Jazz Band all the way from the heart of Devon had arrived and were 'warming up'. They're a fun band with a great repertoire of Jazz classics who were there to get the afternoon swinging. The garden was already busy and as I jumped in the car, I heard the band strike up with 'Alexander's Rag Time Band'; what a lovely 'noise' they made.

Tim and his crew had moved the Blue Dart 120 onto the mooring and had already left to pick up

The Lady Georgina from Compton. I suddenly had the urge to call Julie, "the party's in full swing already up here, what are you up to this afternoon"? "Busy writing up a few articles for The Breeze and I've started putting the Ricky story together, so I'm busy busy, that is unless you've got something on to tempt me away"! I told her where I was headed and asked her to come up later when Pippa would be home. Julie and Pippa had been close as thieves at school and had kept in touch on Facebook ever since. "We'll start the evening at the garden party and finish off in the bash in town", she had said. The Garden Party had always been seen as the event for the 'more mature' whilst the Regatta Night Out with its host of 60's and 70's bands got the Regatta off to a swinging start.

Pippa was certainly a picture when we walked into the garden, she had changed her image with a stunning new look, slimmer, and the long flowing hair had been replaced with a new shorter creation. She turned a few heads, especially those that remembered her as a chubby schoolgirl. Many had seen her on television at the weekend performing in the Albert Hall with the BBC Symphony Orchestra at one of the Henry Wood Prom Concerts.

There were hundreds of people milling around the garden eating, drinking and generally relaxing in the afternoon sun. The hogs were being devoured at an alarming rate and the huge mounds of fresh raspberries and strawberries served with mountains of Devon Clotted Cream were a hit as usual, even though most of the people eating them could ill afford any further clogging of their arteries.

All of a sudden, it suddenly went quiet, even the band stopped playing, it almost felt as if Royalty had arrived and everyone turned to see what was happening. I saw Tim arrive with Georgina on the terrace, she had such a presence about her which almost made people audibly gasp. She had the beauty of a young Princess Diana with the grace of The Queen Mother, she was however a 'thoroughly modern Millie' with an infectious giggle and Tim beside her had a perpetual smile on his face. Pippa and I greeted and welcomed her almost as if she was already family, and she introduced us to her father and mother, The Earl and Lady Compton who had not been expected, leaving both mother and father a little flustered, but Grandma immediately took charge of the situation, with The Earl Langham by her side, another surprise.

This year's party had certainly begun with a real Royal flavour with both families related to The Royal Family. Shock over, the garden resumed its bustle and a general feeling of a 'right royal banquet' ensued almost with the expectancy of jousts and scenes of heraldry amongst the banners and bungees flying in the warm breeze. I saw Julie talking to

Pippa, picked up three glasses of Champagne from the waitress and joined them. There were more than thirty highly prized works of art to auction and at least another thirty high value items going under the hammer, so with the band taking a deserved bar break, the bidding started. Father had admired an excellent river scene in oils by one of Dartmouth's most celebrated artists and there had been fierce bidding for it forcing him to part with more than eleven thousand pounds to secure it for Hawley, with some of the competition coming from his own brother, much to father's annoyance. At the end, the auction had raised more than a hundred and ten thousand pounds for local charities, a record by a large margin, thanks to Grandma and The Earl who seemed to be paying her more attention than was considered appropriate in public, much to mother and father's surprise, even managing to upstage Tim and Georgina.

The fireworks from Hawley's vantage, reflecting on the still waters of the river below against the dying embers of a scarlet sky was a fitting climax to the garden party. Julie and I were still enjoying the bands' final tribute to New Orleans with a 'Moon River' which seemed to bring us closer with each step.

As the evening wore on there were signs of a most spectacular sunset, an orange hue with deep crimson, edged with an even deeper purple. The towns' lights were coming on, along with all of the riverside decorative lighting installed for Regatta, and Dartmouth twinkled like a star against a red velvet sky, Devon's jewel.

Chapter 12

Ricky had been planning his dash for freedom for hours. He knew there would only be one opportunity and even that was a longshot. The penalty for failure would be severe, but he just had to do something. He had sheepishly crawled up the cellar steps to a slightly wider step at the top where the door opened outwards and away from him into possibly a hallway. He positioned himself in a crouching pose with the rail in his left hand and thought that if he could launch himself as soon as the door opened, with the advantage of surprise, he would hit his captor low and attempt to throw him down the steps. Timing would be crucial especially with at least two men to contend with and also, he had no idea of the layout of the house or where the outside door was. He crept back down the steps and sat on the bed. All he had was a blanket and he knew that it would be painful to run very far outside without something to protect his feet.

It was still pitch black in his cell but he felt around the bed frame for a sharp edge that would cut his blanket. His plan was to use part of the blanket to make himself some crude Bootee's, with the remainder wrapped around his waist to protect his vulnerable bits. He could still hear two voices above and the occasional banging or grinding of metallic objects, and that sickly smell kept returning from time to time. He would have to work quiet as a church mouse, first measuring how much material he needed for his 'Tarzan' like shorts. He found the sharpest part of the frame and started sawing and tearing the first cut. Satisfied that it would be OK for the shorts including some to tie them around his waist, he carried on cutting the remaining part of the blanket in two halves to make his footwear. Stopping frequently when he heard footsteps or when it went quiet above, he was able to use the noise of the generator to mask the sawing. If only he had some light, he'd never realised how difficult it was for a blind person to do the simplest of tasks. He tackled a bootee first, wrapping the material around his foot and cutting it into a crude shoe shape. He tore strips of material to 'lace' the finished article and although it felt fairly comfortable walking around the cellar he knew it would offer little protection outside. Satisfied with his efforts but knowing the end result probably looked hideous, he started on the other foot. The 'shorts' proved easier and he was quite proud of himself when he managed to lace a belt through to tie his waist and he even created a supportive crotch to support his 'crown jewels'. He dressed in his new wardrobe and it felt remarkably comfortable, he even seemed warmer and it had the effect of boosting his confidence and self-respect. His efforts had taken what seemed hours and he was quite exhausted. He was complacently congratulating himself on a job well done when he heard a car pull up and its engine switched off. He felt around the bed once more to see if there was any chance of making a weapon of some sorts, but without tools, it was hopeless. He heard a door open and footsteps walk away to his right and towards his position, so he determined that he would turn right at the top of the steps and hopefully find an outside door on his left.

He crept up the steps and took up his crouching position on the top step noting the door opened from right to left which was good. His heart was beating 'ten to the dozen' and he was sweating for the first time in days, probably in fear, because he was also shaking. He didn't know how long he could keep up this position as he could feel tinges of cramping, but just as he thought of moving, he heard footsteps approaching the door, first the bottom bolt pulled then the top bolt.

Here goes, he thought, no backing out now, the door opened and he launched himself with force and hit his captor just above knee height, crashing him into a wall behind him, a tray went flying and before the man recovered, Ricky had grabbed his shirt and sliding slightly to his right had caught him off balance, he pulled with all his might and launched him head first down the steps into the cellar, closed and managed to throw one bolt, he took off, glanced to his right and caught a glimpse of Nina and a man coming for him almost as if it was all happening in slow motion. He hadn't contemplated finding a locked door, but luckily the key was in the lock, he fumbled a little but managed to turn the key and knob in one movement just as the man was a couple of paces away.

He sprinted out of the house with no idea where he was or which way to go. It was dark outside, almost as dark as his prison cellar, but at least his eyes were conditioned to the darkness. He spotted a path slightly ahead and to the left and raced for it, realising too late that it was a rocky and uneven obstacle course leading down to what he now realised was a small beach and the sea. The rocks and stones were tearing at his feet, he tumbled a few times giving his pursuer the advantage but as he fell again, he felt a presence very close, looked over his shoulder and saw that he would have to put up a fight, because he was almost on top of him. He pulled himself upright, grabbed a large pebble and threw it hitting him square on his shoulder which slowed his advance. To Ricky's dismay, he could now see a second shadow descending the path. Nina must have released him from the cellar, and now his troubles were about to multiply for he noticed that he had a length of metal the size of a baseball bat. He picked up two more pebbles, threw them with as much energy as he could muster, turned and spotted the dinghy on the beach, picked up his pace to try and reach it but realised it was a fatal mistake. Before he even made the dinghy, he felt a searing pain as the bar was struck hard across his back, and before he could get back on his feet, another vicious blow smashed into his abdomen along with a boot to the head. Both men were towering above him now, raining blow after blow, kick after kick, punch after punch to his body, legs and face. The world was fading and blackness descended, his body became still and lifeless the fight beaten out of him.

They picked him up like an old sack, one on either side and dragged him back up the path to the cottage, down the steps and threw him onto the bed where he again became a prisoner, but hurting and utterly without hope. The door slammed shut, the bolts thrown and total blackness became his world again.

The family had moved into Hawley's Great Room and drinks were flowing, with the mood jubilant following the success of the garden party. Mother looked up and invited Julie and I to join them for dinner which Mrs Harman was busy preparing. Uncle Nathan and family, Grandma and Pippa along with mother and father were the only ones left in the house with Tim and Georgina out to dinner with her parents and the Earl having made his retreat across the river to Langham. Grandma was being severely teased about the Earl's apparent flirtation and she seemed to be enjoying the attention.

"Julie and I are going down to the Regatta Party in the marquee at Coronation Park, maybe Pippa, Amanda and Oliver would like to join us"? I suggested. The girls jumped at it with Oliver seemingly in some alcoholic daze muttering a reluctant acceptance. Julie's got her car here but she's going home first, we could get a taxi there and back as I'm sure it's a boozy do which seemed to greatly cheer Oliver up.

I walked Julie to the car and sat in the passenger seat with her. "You're not coming down now are you Bobby"? she said surprised. "No Julie, I want to talk to you. I feel so guilty with everyone having a great time but poor old Ricky held in some grotty hole somewhere". "I know" she said, "but what can we do"? "Well", I said, "I have a theory that the sailboat, Poppet has something to do with it and I want to take a looksee tonight". "I thought we were all going to the bash in town," she said. "What I'd like to do is after the party, take Pilgrim's tender out of the river and round to Scabbacombe so I can take a closer look at her". "That's a hell of a risk Bobby, what if they are holding Ricky on-board, there will surely be someone guarding him". "That is a possibility, but I just have to satisfy my curiosity". I'm coming with you, no arguments, I can help hold the tender steady while you climb on-board, besides, it's my story so I need to be there to get the facts straight". This was Julie at her most forceful and I knew that I had already lost the argument. Julie left having arranged to meet up at the jetty at ten, and I left to gather some tools and anything I might need for tonight's adventure.

I saw Pippa on the stairway and told her I had arranged a taxi for nine thirty but that I would meet them there. Showered and changed, I made my way down to the marina and boarded Pilgrim to take her onto the town jetty for the night. Julie was waiting on the pontoon and took my lines. We secured her and she came on-board and left her crew bag on the starboard bunk. Dartmouth was still full of bustle following the fireworks and the street traders were making a rare killing on a beautiful August evening.

We made our way along the Quay to the sound of distant music from the marquee. It was heaving with a great atmosphere and the joy of sharing some of the best party music from the 60's and 70's played by some of Devon's best tribute acts. The bar was three deep but it was a meeting of friends who hadn't seen each other since school days but returned to the reunion each year. Both young and old seemed to relate to that golden age of The Beatles, The Kinks, Mungo Jerry and the Beach

Boys with the dance floor was packed all through the night. Time seemed to fly and before anyone realised it, 'Save the last dance for me' by an authentic Engelbert Humperdink was bringing the shindig to a close. Oliver had passed out, face down on one of the tables and it took a huge effort by all of us to get him on his feet, staggering to the waiting taxi on the quay. Julie and I serenaded arm in arm back to Pilgrim.

We were both pretty sober despite having more to drink than we had planned but we were still determined to see this mission through. We both changed into dark clothing, I added a night torch with a red glow to the bag of tools I had and we slipped quietly into the dinghy, pushed away and rowed downriver in a slack tide before firing up the outboard opposite the castle. The sea was calm with just a light chop and although I had been out on Pilgrim many a time rounding The Mew Stone, it seemed strange to be out there in a small dinghy with Julie on-board. Within twenty minutes we had cut the engine and I was again rowing just in case the engine was heard as we approached Poppet.

The boat was in total darkness, swinging on her anchor but as we came closer we could see a light in the cottage. I looked at my watch, it was almost two o'clock. "Someone's having a late night" I whispered, "maybe they were at the same party as us" she said. Unlikely, I thought if my intuition was right. We carefully manoeuvred close without touching Poppet's hull, I tied us off and Julie held the dinghy off whilst I carefully climbed aboard. She creaked and the halyard slapped the mast, I froze but there was no movement. The companionway hatch was closed but didn't look locked. With my night torch in one hand, I slid open the cover and pulled one of the hatchway doors ajar, again there was no movement so I opened it wide and shone the red beam into the saloon. It was a mess, no sailor would keep their boat in such chaos. I lowered myself carefully down the companionway ladder and checked out the aft berth which was full of junk but little of interest. The saloon was also a mess with dirty mugs and plates in the galley sink. The V-berth was surprisingly tidy which suggested someone was or had used it to sleep. I checked the head which was also disgusting, the whole area below stunk with a rancid choking stench. I checked out the navigation table, the only clues on the charts I was already aware of, the coordinates for the rendezvous the previous night. There was a light tap on the hull and I stuck my head out of the companionway, Julie whispered that the light had gone out in the cottage but she had seen no other movement. "I've finished anyway" I said and closed the two hatch doors, slid the cover back in position and dropped back into the dinghy.

We pushed off and I rowed until the cottage was out of sight before firing up the outboard and heading back to Pilgrim. "Maybe I am wrong and those people are just tourists in Devon for August" I said pulling up at the jetty. We didn't speak much as there were other boats tied up and their crews would be asleep at two thirty in the morning. I walked Julie back to her flat, we kissed passionately and I was desperate for an invite upstairs, but it was late, not the right time, so said I'd call her in the morning and returned to Pilgrim to crash. I climbed aboard, opened the hatchway, lowered myself down into the large comfortable saloon and closed the hatch. Damn, I thought, I should have asked Julie to stay on-board with me.

I switched on the light in the galley to make myself a mug of tea and it was then I felt a presence, a shiver went down my back. I had my back to the darkened saloon, I turned and saw the silhouette of a man sitting facing me on the couch. "What the hell, who are you and what are you doing on my boat", I approached him rather aggressively not thinking that he may have some sort of weapon. He stood and I saw he was a large fit looking man and stopped in my tracks when he lifted his hand in a defensive gesture, "Mr Hawley, my name is Matthew Kinder, I work for Sir Michael Gilbert and I just want to talk to you". "You've got a cheek, what the hell do you think you're doing breaking into my boat at this time of night"? "I've been watching you for a couple of days, trawling the river in your dinghy on Monday, disappearing offshore in your boat last night and sneaking off with your flusey, Julie Fairbrother again in the dead of night, it is very suspicious behaviour Mr Hawley". "How dare you call her my flusey, Julie and I have done more to try and find Ricky than anyone, including the police, and for you to even suggest that we may be involved in his disappearance is ridiculous". I turned, went to the hatchway and opened it, stood and indicated he should leave immediately. He hesitated but realised he had made a mistake and climbed the companionway ladder. "If you come near me or Julie Fairbrother, or my boat again Mr Kinder, I will throw you overboard and put DS Morgan on to you". I closed and bolted the hatchway behind him and watched as he climbed down on to the jetty and make his way back up to the Quay. I was still shaking, more from anger than fear, why an intelligent and wealthy man like Sir Michael had hired this idiot I had no idea, but I would phone Elizabeth in the morning to find out.

Chapter 13

There was a loud tapping on the hull which stirred me from a deep sleep. The clock on the bulkhead said six thirty and I cursed at the intrusion especially after a heavy day and night. I unlocked the hatchway and stuck my bleary head through to see an unsmiling Sam the Harbourmaster glaring at me. "Now you should know better Bobby than to give me problems on the first day of Regatta". I suddenly realised what the matter was, I should have moved off the jetty before six when the river ferries start to operate, and with the river traffic higher still this morning of all mornings, I could understand why Sam was upset. "Sorry Sam, heavy night at the party last night and I forgot to set an alarm, I'll be underway in less than five minutes". Sam shook his head, more as a gesture of an acceptance that the young of today had no sense of responsibility. I shot back through the hatch, pulled on last night's clothes and emerged utterly dishevelled onto the dock to release my spring lines. I'd started the diesel, the tide was ebbing, which naturally moved Pilgrim's bows off the jetty, released the aft line and in less than the time it took to shake a hand, I was motoring back to Sand Quay. I raised a hand to Sam who acknowledged my swift exit with a nod and a wink.

I never liked getting up early but I loved being up early, there was a magic to the river early in the morning, before the regular traffic disturbed the tranquillity. The mist was just rising with the warmth of the sun's rays, giving the whole river an eerie feeling. I weaved between the moored boats out into the main channel and saw a huge behemoth of a cruise ship being guided in by the pilot boat. Dartmouth regularly welcomed cruise ships, some of the modern vessels so large that they had to reverse up the river as it wasn't wide enough for them to turn. The ship was the MS Balmoral, a regular visitor, especially for Regatta week, with up to twelve hundred passengers adding to the towns' wealth and atmosphere. I slowed Pilgrim down so that I could watch the Captain manoeuvre the vessel between the two largest mooring buoys in the centre of the river, downstream from HMS Somerset, a skill that never ceased to amaze me. Excitement over, I headed home and was back at the marina in no time, docked, with Pilgrim tied off before going up to the hall to freshen up and change for breakfast.

Ricky was also shaken out of his semi-conscious slumber by his captors. He felt as if every bone in his body had been broken, his face ached and despite the light being on, he could hardly make out the two men towering above him through swollen and painful eyes. They lifted him clean off the bed and slammed him into the wall, he screamed with pain and although he began to slide to the ground, his legs seemingly incapable of supporting him, they again lifted him. He stood long enough for them to take another damned picture and then threw him back on to the bed without a word being spoken, left the room, bolted the door and returned him into his customary darkness. He was sure several ribs were broken and he was worried his sight might be damaged. He ran his hands over his face and other parts of his body and could feel scabs and dried up blood, some wounds still either weeping or bleeding and very painful. The generator was still humming above so his hearing seemed intact, but when he tried to move into a more comfortable position he almost passed out so severe was the pain around his rib cage.

Within an hour, the picture and email had pinged into Michael's inbox, it read:

"To Sir Michael Gilbert, your son has suffered punishment for the sins of his father, and as a direct result of your refusal to comply with our explicit instructions. Any further transgressions will result in his death. If you want to see your son alive again you will transfer the six million pounds in bitcoins to the following address:

"31uEbMgunupShBVTewXjtqbBv5MndwfXhb"

The transfer to be completed no later than midnight tomorrow, Friday. There will be no further communication".

Michael called Ted into his office and closed the door. "Ted, I want your advice, I've had another of those ghastly emails and it looks as if Ricky's in a really bad way". He turned his computer screen so that Ted could see an almost unrecognisable picture of Ricky, his face looking as if he'd been in the ring with Tyson and his swollen body covered in cuts and bruises. Ted was shocked, his immediate thought was that these people, whoever they were had inflicted unnecessary torture on his nephew. Ted was so shocked he hadn't uttered a word. "They're animals, I can't show this to Ellen, Ted, it will break her heart, and I wish I could get him out of there sooner, but George has been helping me with this bitcoin thing and the problem is that finding an exchange that can handle this large amount before tomorrow. The account is open and the sterling is available but we can't seem to get the transaction completed until late tomorrow as it will take that long for the funds to clear". Ted had no intelligent suggestions, "I can't believe, judging by what they've done that it's a local gang, I've seen pictures like these in The Foreign Office of hostages held in Iraq and Somalia and the like, they will not negotiate and seem to take pleasure in inflicting pain. Have the police come back with anything yet"? "Nothing, they're convinced there's a 'mole' either in the household or estate staff. They've checked out the house and think it's clear but the problem with the estate is the hundreds of temporary staff employed at this time of year in the orchards and vineyard, let alone on the estate's arable farms.

I do have one other card up my sleeve, I used a Private Investigator a couple of years ago to check out an employee who I suspected of passing sensitive information about our drones to our competitors, and he managed to flush him out, so I've secretly brought him in. Last I heard from him was that he was following a particular lead which he felt confident would yield something, so I have at least a little hope remaining".

The phone rang and Michael answered, "Can I speak to Sir Michael please", "speaking" he replied. "Sir" I said, "it's Bobby Hawley, am I right in saying that you have employed a Private Investigator named Matthew Kinder to look for Ricky"? Michael was flabbergasted and the question momentarily flustered him. "Why do you ask, Bobby"? "Last night, Matthew Kinder broke into my boat, Pilgrim, and accused Julie Fairbrother and I of being involved in Ricky's disappearance, and this morning he has stalked Julie whilst she was walking her dog and put the fear of God into her. I'm with her now and she is extremely upset, and frankly Sir Michael, your man is an amateur who seems to believe that the two people who are actively trying to find Ricky, who is after all our friend, of somehow being involved. I have a good mind to go to DS Morgan and make a formal complaint". "Don't do that Bobby, I don't want this to become public knowledge, and I apologise unreservedly for the intrusion and implication. I know you are close to both Ricky and especially Elizabeth. I'm sorry and I will urgently have strong words with him". He hung up, "what was all that about"? Ted asked. "It seems my confidence in my investigator has just taken a tumble, it looks as if he's been barking up the wrong tree and upsetting our friends and neighbours".

Julie had confronted a man she suspected of following her up to the castle, and according to the staff in the cafe, had seen him off in no uncertain terms. She had called me afterwards and had gone into a bit of a meltdown, the cafe owner had sat her down with a strong cup of tea until I arrived. I had brought Julie and Rusty home to Hawley and she was slowly recovering. "I thought it was one of those men again Bobby, but I gave him a piece of my mind, but couldn't stop shaking once he'd gone". I had brought her home knowing that she would settle down, especially with Pippa there, and she had calmed down enough to join us for breakfast on the terrace in the morning sun.

Michael had spoken very harshly to Matthew Kinder and when he realised that Bobby and Julie were his only 'hot' leads, had 'read him the riot act' and told him he needed to up his game and come up with something credible within 24 hours, also warning him that he could not afford this going public for Ricky's sake. He knew he was fast running out of options and concentrated on organising the finances with no guarantee that Ricky would be released even when he did pay the ransom. Michael had never felt so out of control his entire life, Ted's political and counter-intelligence people had been little help and the police virtually useless. He again called on his father, hoping The Earl's counsel would provide some inspiration as to what could be done in the very little time they had left.

Ellen and Elizabeth were blissfully unaware of the latest developments, and although their thoughts were never far from Ricky's plight, they were occupying their minds with the list of things to do for the Regatta Ball in two days. All the marquees were now in place, some used for storage and preparation of cold and chilled foods, which were kept fresh in cold rooms powered by two large generators which had been installed and commissioned. The large marquee had its flooring laid and staging for the orchestra and a large dance floor. Lighting and floral decorations were being placed and the large round tables for ten had been set out with a bar area to complete the layout. They had employed professionals to organise everything down to the last detail and they were sat around one of the tables arranging estate staff who had volunteered for the varied duties to be filled on the night, with some allocated to car parking duties, cloakroom staff, waiters and waitresses at tables, bar staff and security to ensure that only those that had purchased the ninety five pounds a head ticket could attend. The whole garden area was a hive of activity and it kept the housekeeper, Ellen and Elizabeth very busy organising the minute details. Even the drive down from Langham's grand gates to the house and beyond down the hill to the river dockage were being swept clean by a gang of estate workers.

Over at Hawley, Julie had recovered from her morning ordeal and was laughing and giggling with Pippa and mother. Father and Tim had left after breakfast to greet the first of their list of clients taking a tour of the Blue Dart 120. The yacht was already sold to a wealthy Turkish businessman who was arriving on Saturday to inspect his new toy but in the meantime, he had agreed to allow the yard to show it to invited guests both at the Regatta and at next month's Southampton Boat Show before we were scheduled to deliver her to Gibraltar for his crew to take her across the Mediterranean.

Even Rusty had settled down after his morning encounter, having apparently barked continuously at Matthew Kinder. Rusty had been treated with some of Blackie and Barney's favourite biscuits, and they were romping around the garden like mad things. An idea popped into my head, "why don't we take the dogs for a good old walk, I could do with stretching my legs and besides, I'm not needed down on the boat until this afternoon. The girls jumped at it and I was sure the dogs would be equally thrilled, but I had an ulterior motive which I didn't share with the girls. I joked with Pippa that lungful's of sea air would do her some good after breathing in that polluted London stuff in order to get them into the car for a short journey first.

The dogs jumped in the back of my Range Rover and I headed down the long Hawley drive and out onto the road towards Brixham. I turned on to narrow Slappers Hill at Hillhead and parked off the road at the Coleton Fishacre turnoff. The girls couldn't figure where I was taking them, but no sooner than the dogs were out of the back, they spotted the public footpath signposted to the SW Coast Path and no further questions were asked! The path led down through Nethway Wood and across to Woodhuish before picking up Scabbacombe Lane down to the path. The morning was bright sunshine with wispy white cloud and a gentle Southerly breeze off the sea. We turned left towards Scabbacombe Cottage with Julie tugging at my sleeve and making eyes at me in a "are you mad" sort of way. I had figured that nobody would suspect two girls and a chap with three dogs, and anyway I had only intended going to within view of the cottage to satisfy my curiosity and establish whether a plan that was developing in my head was feasible. The girls were chatting away incessantly, with Pippa oblivious as to why we were walking this particular route. Poppet was the first to come into view, anchored in the cove, followed by the roof of Scabbacombe Cottage, we had been walking for about an hour before I could see that the cottage was quiet with no car parked, but the dinghy was pulled up on the beach just as I had seen it before. Without going too close, I suggested doing a circular route via Coleton Fishacre back to the car, and the girls who were still talking ten to the dozen dutifully agreed.

We were back at Hawley in time for lunch and the walk had made us really hungry, which was good, because there was a mountain of food left over from the Garden Party, and I was looking forward to tucking in to some cold Hogg and pickle followed by some raspberries and clotted cream. Julie and I left shortly afterwards, and used one of the buggies to go down to the marina as I needed the tender to transport my two guests across to the Regatta 65. Once we were away from the house, Julie looked at me suspiciously, "and what are you planning now Bobby Hawley"? "I'm convinced that Scabbacombe holds the key to Ricky's disappearance, that was just a reconnaissance mission to see whether we could find an opportunity to get closer, when maybe Poppet moves the next time". Although Julie had freaked at being accosted alone, she was determined to help find Ricky. "You're on" she had said as we climbed into the tender with Rusty more interested in getting into the water than into the boat. I dropped Julie off at the town dock and crossed over to the motor yacht to join father and Tim.

Chapter 14

The Royal Regattas' opening ceremony had taken place with the customary procession from the Guildhall headed by the Mayor in full regalia. There were speeches and the Town Crier had officially declared the Regatta 'open'. It was as much a spectacle for the visitors as it was the tradition, which had started when Queen Victoria had unexpectedly visited in 1856 along with Prince Albert and the Prince of Wales and granted the Regatta Royal Patronage. The rowing events were well underway with skulls and whaler crews battling it out against an incoming tide. The quayside was thronged with spectators, cheering and clapping the boats as they passed. Day trippers arriving in dozens of coaches were mingling with hoards of German and American tourists off the Balmoral and they were further swelled by hundreds crossing the river by ferry having arrived on the Steam Trains of the Dartmouth Steam Railway and Riverboat Company. There was music from the bandstand, the street market was in full swing and a tug of war event was scheduled later in the afternoon, which was inevitably going to be won by either the local rugby team or the Royal Navy, or maybe there was an outside chance that one of the local pubs might put up an outstanding performance. In any event it would be entertaining especially since one of the teams entered was from the local constabulary with DS Morgan as the anchor man at the back, and the sailing club team with George and me. It was every team's ambition to beat the police. Last year's event was a hilarious mud bath, especially when one joker in the rugby club team had reduced his team members to bellyfuls of laughter by declaring during the bout that he didn't mind coming last, as long as he beat the police.

In the meantime, Morgan had been summoned to Langham to meet with The Earl and Sir Michael to discuss Ricky's kidnapping. They both regretted not having contacted him earlier but had shown him the email messages and pictures so that he would at least understand why they had not. With only little over 24 hours left they were willing to listen to any plan he may have to find Ricky, but Morgan only had one suggestion, which was very risky. He admitted that his small force had no leads, but made an unprecedented suggestion, that they contract the national TV networks to air the story on the six o'clock news. Whilst he admitted that it might endanger Ricky's life, it might also jog somebody's memory of something or someone they may have seen. There were gasps of disbelief from both men and much shaking of heads. Frankly, Morgan would have been surprised if they'd gone for it.

"In truth, we only have one other line of enquiry at present and I am a little embarrassed that it isn't a police operation at all, and had therefore decided not to share it with you, but if I can rely on it staying between these four walls, I am willing to put you in the picture". Both men nodded their agreement and were willing to do almost anything to help get Ricky back safely. "You know Bobby Hawley and Julie Fairbrother"? They both looked astonished and explained the Matthew Kinder connection to Morgan, which as it turned out, he was already aware of. "Before I continue it is only fair to tell you that we have given Mr Kinder a bit of a scare and a warning, mainly to protect Bobby and Julie, because frankly, he was making a bit of a nuisance of himself". "That's a bit unfair Mr Morgan, because we believe that Matthew Kinder had come to the same conclusion as you have". "No, that would be the wrong conclusion", Morgan continued, "the exact opposite in fact. You are probably not aware that it was Bobby who first realised that there was more to Ricky's disappearance than just some booze and a girl or two. Bobby was the one who found your tender with blood on a lifejacket and he brought a picture and the jacket to me on Sunday night, before the first email was sent to you". They both drew closer and were now eager to learn more. "Since that night, Bobby especially, and sometimes Julie, who clearly sees a newspaper story in the offing, have been acting strangely and disappearing at all hours of the night". He explained that he had one of his plain clothes officers keep an eye on Bobby especially, and he told them the story when the both of them got in his dinghy at almost two in the morning the night before. "Why don't you pull them in for questioning then"? was their inevitable question. "Whilst I'm bloody annoyed with them, especially Bobby, and believe you me, I'd like to give him a right old roasting, I think they're on to something and at the moment, I prefer to keep a distance and be there to assist them if and when they need it". They all agreed it was a hell of a longshot and a gamble with Ricky's life, but Morgan advised them to delay the ransom payment as long as they could to give this slender hope a bit of a chance. "Where are they now"? Michael asked. "Bobby's working on their two new fancy yachts on the river, taking clients for cocktails I expect and trying to fill their order books. Have you seen those two beauties, I wish I had the money to afford one of those Gin Palaces, but not a chance on a policeman's salary"? "What about Julie"? "Bobby dropped her off earlier and she's at home as far as we know". There was nothing more to discuss so Morgan shook hands with two dubious looking men and headed back to the station to catch up on some paperwork before gathering up his team for the tug of war.

The Regatta 65 was sold to an American from Fort Lauderdale. He needed a large comfortable sailboat with a shallow draft to negotiate the waters from the Bahamas to Key West, yet he also wanted stability on long ocean crossings. This boat was unique and I was demonstrating its hydraulic centreboard, which changed its draft from a shallow four foot six to nine feet at the touch of a button. Like the larger motor yacht, she was fitted out to the highest standards in the best quality English oak and calf leather upholstery. We had just returned to the mooring after a short sail into Start Bay and the owner and three other clients, two Brits and an Italian were head over heels in love with her. The American wanted to sail her back across the Atlantic immediately, but we had an agreement to show her in Southampton before he could get his mitts on her.

Father had come over to the sailboat and had invited them to come aboard the Blue Dart for some refreshments and to watch the Breitling Aerobatic Wing Walking Team due to entertain in an hours' time. I had taken the opportunity to change and join my sailing club team mates for what would be a fun hour of tug of war.

I made my way up to Coronation Park where Morgan sneaked up and slapped me on the back with enough force to dislocate a shoulder, "ready to face the might of the 'men in blue then Bobby"? We had unfortunately drawn them in the first round and were expected to lose. First, we watched the team from The Royal Castle get hammered by the Crab and Bucket pub team, and they were followed by an even match between the Royal Navy from Britannia College and Dartmouth Rugby Club who eventually took the honours. Our match against the local police was a laughable display, very one-sided in our favour and the police had retreated to chants of "who ate all the pies". The whole event was held in a great spirit of comradery which had eventually seen the Rugby Club victorious.

Julie had brought Rusty up to Coronation Park and had shouted herself almost hoarse, Rusty too had got into the spirit of the event and barked every time Julie cheered. I had no problem persuading her that a drink was desperately needed. We walked over to the Dartmouth Arms and settled down with the drinks in Bayards Cove to watch the Breitling Wing Walkers aerobatic display. They performed gymnastics and dance on the wings of their planes whilst the pilots put them through rolls, loops, stall turns and even inverted flying, all at a dizzying hundred and fifty miles an hour, sometimes barely above the water. The Balmoral passengers arguably had the best vantage high above the river, a fantastic end to their visit to Dartmouth, for no sooner than the display had finished, she slowly made her way down the river to her next destination, but there would be nowhere surely that could touch the beauty or the excitement of Dartmouth on Regatta week.

I remembered I owed Julie a dinner and asked if she was game, not even knowing whether I would stand a chance of a table anywhere tonight. Taylor's was fully booked but I managed to get a reservation in the Royal Castle's restaurant. It was such a warm evening, we had another drink before arranging to call for her at seven thirty to walk over to The Castle.

I made my way back to the quay and bumped into Elizabeth and her mother who had escaped Langham to support George in one of the sculls rowing events and to watch the aerobatic display. I was always uncomfortable in Ellen's company, it was as if she knew that Elizabeth and I had more than a platonic relationship, and she couldn't help herself from showing her disapproval, even now, when Elizabeth was engaged. Ellen saw a couple she knew and was only too eager to move away from me, which gave Elizabeth a chance to talk. "Bobby, I'm so glad I bumped into you, it's almost a week since Ricky went missing and Daddy says the police are no further forward in finding him. Tomorrow is the day we have to pay the ransom, but there's no guarantee they'll let him go even when we do. We're so afraid we'll never see him again". She began to cry, and I put my arms around her to give some comfort but was immediately aware of an unfriendly glare from Ellen, but chose to ignore her silly attitude. I thought friends were always there for each other and Elizabeth was old enough to choose hers. "Be brave Elizabeth, all is not lost yet, you know what they say, it's not over until the fat lady sings, there is still hope". It was a feeble attempt to comfort her, there was nothing more I could say, but as I returned to the tender, I felt even more determined to see our plan through in the morning.

Uncle Nathan was making a beeline for me, "Bobby old chap, glad I caught you, are those the two new beauties out in the river", referring to the yards' latest creations. "Yes Uncle, has nobody taken you across yet for the tour"? Oliver still had that sullen look about him and had no interest in coming, and I have to admit to being a little cruel for not mentioning the free champagne and canapés, knowing he'd walk on water for free food and drink. Aunt Margaret and Amanda jumped at the chance and I took the three of them over to the motor yacht before making my way back to Sand Quay and home.

Ricky was aware of a lot of movement above, footsteps going through the door and even what he thought was noise outside. A car door was being closed from time to time as if they were carrying things from the house. Having escaped outside, he had a better idea of the layout around the house, but he still had no idea where he was except that it was somewhere on the coast. Were they getting ready to vacate or move him somewhere else, but he also had a dark thought that his number might be up. He almost jumped out of his skin when the bolts rattled and the door opened. Although he had seen a glimpse of their faces in the dark when he'd made a run for it, they still wore hoods. He braced himself for another assault on his body, but was relieved when they brought some food and a drink and even a blanket. No words were spoken, but they did leave the light on long enough for him to eat. He heard the outside door close again and the lock turn, his light went out but the generator remained humming away, but there was no other sound.

     Morgan was back in his office following the humiliation of their tug of war defeat. He was pouring over bank and credit card statements for Hannah Parker which showed that her last transaction was an online purchase of a single Railway ticket from London Paddington to her mother's home at Paignton over three months earlier. Previous tickets she had purchased were always returns, and Morgan had come to the conclusion that she must have found a local job and was not returning to London. He had secured CCTV footage of the ticket machine on Paddington Station where Hannah had collected her tickets on the afternoon of the third of May. He had watched the footage several times and could not fathom why the CCTV picture bore no resemblance to the picture he had borrowed from her mum's nursing home. He was trying to figure out how her body had been found in Devon if she wasn't the one who'd travelled on the train that day. Had she travelled to Devon with someone, a friend or work colleague who had then murdered her, or was she already dead, but for what reason? He was baffled, and it annoyed him. He hated open cases, and between Hannah and Ricky's disappearance, both frustrated the hell out of him. He had a thought, could the two incidents be linked in some way, although they were three months apart. He had one of those itches he couldn't scratch and began to consider how they could be linked.

I was showered and changed and looking forward to spending the evening with Julie. I jumped in the car with the intention of driving into town but realised I preferred it, and found it easier to take Pilgrim's tender to the town dock; no parking issues and no ferries to negotiate. I parked the car down in the marina car park and jumped in the boat. On the way down, I wondered if Julie would stay on Pilgrim tonight if I could persuade her, it would be easier for an early start in the morning. By the time I was knocking on her door, I had convinced myself it was a good idea but knew she would be harder to persuade. Rusty had to say hello too by putting his paws up on my clean shirt, but luckily, his paws were clean.

Julie was pleased to see me which made my heart leap and we walked over to The Royal Castle arm in arm. As usual, it was heaving, we had half an hour before our table reservation and settled down in the Harbour Bar with my usual pint of Doom Bar and a Vodka Redbull for Julie. Morgan who had called in for a pint on his way home, or so he said had invited himself to sit at our table and instantly made Julie laugh by saying he had called in for some more pies on his way home, "because the missus's cooking was bloody awful". In truth, he was good company and made fun of everything and everyone. But, as usual with Morgan, there was a purpose to his visit, "I'm not sure yet what you two are up to, but I know you are up to something, and I would hazard an educated guess that it has something to do with Ricky's disappearance. I just want you to know that if you need any help, just call me, we've got your back". He downed his pint and rose to leave before we had a chance to say or do anything other than look at each other in disbelief, "good luck, whatever it is" he said, and gave us a wink. "Enjoy your dinner too" he added, and left. We were both speechless for what seemed an age. "How the hell did Morgan know we were having a meal here" Julie asked. "More's to the point, was he bluffing or does he know something, and if he does, how"?

Our table was ready and we followed the waitress upstairs into the restaurant which was full to the rafters. In the light of the restaurant, I could not take my eyes off Julie who was dressed in a simple thigh length salmon cotton dress, a heavy turquoise and silver necklace with matching bangle, and simple turquoise leather shoulder bag finished off with shoes to match. She turned every male head in the restaurant and a few admiring glances from their respective partners. Julie seemed to be able to transform herself from an outwardly tomboyish day to day look into a ravishing beauty with the simplest of outfits and the minimal of effort. Sitting across from me, I realised how natural our relationship was, so unlike the rather starchy and impersonal nature of Elizabeth's demeanour to the utterly laid back and relaxed nature of being with Julie. I suddenly realised I was falling for her, and in a big way. We didn't stop talking to each other the entire evening and were the last to leave, having had another drink in the bar on the way home.

We had walked back to Julie's and she had eagerly agreed to spend the night on-board Pilgrim with me, on one condition, that Rusty came too. We had quickly gone up to Julie's flat for her to pack for the morning and pick up some food for Rusty, and we had joyfully made our way to the tender, Rusty in tow. It was remarkably quiet on the river and even Smugglers Landing was in darkness. I lifted Rusty onto Pilgrim's transom and helped Julie aboard, opened the hatch and turned some cosy lights on in the saloon. I was flabbergasted to see the clock on the bulkhead said thirty minutes past midnight. Julie declined a nightcap and a tea so I showed her into the aft stateroom. I had intended to make tracks at dawn which was less than six hours away, we looked at each other with desire in both our eyes, but it was Julie who broke the spell and suggested we should get some rest, which in truth I agreed, besides, the timing was just not right for our first intimate moment, even though I wanted her with every sinew in my body. We kissed and I left to use the starboard stateroom, set the alarm for five thirty and closed my eyes with both Julie and Ricky on my mind.

Chapter 15

Scabbacombe Cottage was a hive of activity a couple of hours before dawn. Mo and Karin had wrapped the cider barrel in a couple of heavy duty black refuse bags and were in the process of carrying it down the rugged path to the beach. When Nina had opened the door, she had been surprised to see a dramatic change in the weather with a dense, cold sea mist rolling in. She could hardly see her hand in front of her face which would make the trip a lot slower and more difficult but not impossible. They carefully carried the now heavier barrel down to the beach whilst Nina dragged the dinghy into the water.

They safely placed the barrel in the centre and Mo and Nina walked the dinghy into deeper water before getting in and rowing out to Poppet, although they still couldn't see her, the mist swirling, blanketing land and sea. Karin had already slipped out of sight and gone back to the cottage. Nina rowed whilst Mo kept his eyes peeled for the boat. Although they had made this trip many times before, the mist was disorientating them and they were in fear of over shooting Poppet altogether. Mo spotted a dark shadow through the mist and directed Nina's efforts towards it, and there she was, Poppet swinging on her anchor, the relief in the dinghy was palpable. Nina tied off and stepped aboard whilst Mo, very carefully lifted the barrel over the transom before stepping over the rail himself. Nina had already opened the hatchway and Mo completed his task, securing it in the V deck. Nina started the diesel and fired up her hand held GPS, loaded the marine chart with its breadcrumb trail for their destination up the Dart to the Harbourne River.

Nina was unconcerned about finding the destination with the aid of the GPS but needed to keep a very close watch for other boats in the confined space of the river especially. Nina had hauled two extra radar reflectors onto the spreaders and installed Mo at the pulpit rail, much to his disgust, to keep a lookout and listen for other vessels. In the event, the trip proved unremarkable and they dropped anchor close to Kirkham Copse without incident. The barrel was successfully transferred to the wood and Mo had already prepared a secure hiding place until later in the day. Nina prepared to sail back down the river leaving Mo to get back to his job at the cider mill, although he would need to kill some time as it was still only a little after dawn.

The alarm shook me from deep sleep, the shock nearly tumbling me from my bed. The air felt cooler and damp this morning or was I imagining it. A bright and breezy Julie stuck her head around the door, "tea's up, and I found some cereal in the cupboard and even fresh milk in the fridge, you do keep Pilgrim well stocked", she said. "She's ready to go to sea at a drop of a hat, and come to think of it, I sleep more often on board than I do up at the hall. Now if you don't want a big surprise, close the door and let me get up".

By the time I'd washed and changed, the saloon was cosy and warm, a steaming mug of tea and a bowl of muesli was on the dinette table. Julie looked as if she was taking this mission seriously, dressed in perfect walkers gear, complete with boots and I noted the rucksack with some essentials on the settee. "You're organised this morning" I said, "what in heaven's name have you packed in that rucksack"? "I'm worried what state we'll find Ricky in, he's been gone the best part of a week so I've packed a few things we might need". I had a peep in the rucksack, there were some of my clothes, an old pair of my deck shoes, the first aid kit and cereal bars from my tuck tin. "Where did you find all this stuff" I asked, "quite the Girl Guide aren't we". "Be Prepared, I've never forgotten the Girl Guides motto, besides better to have it with us and not need it than not have it". I had a rucksack of my own with some equally important items, some of which would get me arrested if I was stopped by the police. I'd borrowed a jemmy from the workshop, my sheathed fillet knife and a flare gun with a handful of flares. I opened the hatchway and a rush of much cooler air than of late dropped in. I popped my head outside finding a thick sea mist blanketing the marina. I could hardly make out Pilgrim's bow and the river itself did not exist. It seemed as if we were the only boat in the marina and even the boat sheds and Smugglers Landing were utterly invisible with a swirling damp and eerily quiet dawn still to show itself. I dropped back down into the saloon, "we'll need our light waterproofs this morning and a large flask of coffee won't go amiss either, it's bleak out there and I don't expect it to clear until the sun burns through. I checked the barometer which was still steady indicating no real change in the wonderful summer weather we had been having for the past fortnight.

We checked we had everything, Rusty was ready to come too, I had grown to love that old dog and was becoming a big old softie myself. I lowered the guardrail and before I could stop him, he jumped down onto the pontoon and very nearly fell straight off the other side into the water. As we walked along the pontoon I could hear another pair of footsteps coming towards us, but so was the density of the mist, he didn't come into view until we were almost upon each other. It was our dock master, Dave, "morning boaters, what gets you two up so early on a bleak morning like this"? he said at the top of his voice, forgetting that other mariners were still fast asleep in their bunks. "Early morning walkies for Rusty", I said, who by now had shot past Dave nearly knocking him into the water. Dave was always an early bird, cheerful whether it was early in the morning or late at night, and went about his work enthusiastically checking on the boats to make sure they were secure and their owners safe. "Don't get lost out there" he chirped, "there are some strange happenings around here in the mist, probably the ghosts of the old smugglers. I hear their old bones rattling now and then", he chuckled as he disappeared into the mist and rattled one of the halyards on an unoccupied boat before giving a " ho ho ho and a bottle of rum" rendition. "He's a cheerful bugger in the morning isn't he", Julie remarked as we tried to find my car in the gloom of the car park. "Oh don't take any notice of Dave, he's like that all the time and believe you me, he scares the living daylights out of some of the young lads in the marina with his antics".

We found the car, dumped our rucksacks in the back with Rusty and edged our way out of the car park and up the lane to the main road. I had planned to head straight for Slappers Lane and park where we had the day before and walk through Nethway Wood to the coast path, but with the mist, I figured we would get enough cover if I left the car at Woodhuish and walk down Scabbacombe Lane instead. It is amazing how a thick mist or fog can disorientate you despite knowing an area like the back of your hand, but having taken two wrong turnings, I decided to use technology and entered Woodhuish onto my Satnav before I got completely lost. Woodhuish was not deserted as I expected at this early hour, I had forgotten how early our farmers were up, especially at harvest time, and I had to make way for an enormous combine harvester, which took up the entire lane and clipped both hedges, followed by a tractor pulling a flatbed trailer. I found a suitable place out of sight behind one of the farm buildings to park, we let Rusty out and picked up our rucksacks, making our way down the lane to the turnoff to Scabbacombe.

From the end of the lane, the footpath led down to the coast path, Rusty bounding away ahead of us but Julie and I walking in silence, deep in thought as to the madness of such a venture. Why had I not involved Morgan in this caper kept going through my mind, but I always came back with the same answer, I had no evidence that the people in Scabbacombe Cottage had anything to do with Ricky's disappearance, just a gut feel. The mist was swirling in off the sea and rising up the cliff and sweeping inland. I could hear the sound of the waves breaking at the bottom of the cliff but could see nothing. It was still dark but the mist was taking on a lighter grey to the East. We edged forward towards the coast path which followed the line of the cliffs. It was mostly exposed but where there had been some rock falls, a fence with a warning notice had been erected a few feet away from the edge. Rusty had disappeared again, Julie called but there was no sign of him. "He's probably chasing some rabbits" I suggested, but she called again with more urgency in her voice, and within a few seconds he was back, panting and his tail wagging in excitement. I had checked the map and calculated we were about three quarters of a mile away from the cottage along the coast path. The mist gave us great cover from being seen but made the walk slower and more dangerous. It also stopped me seeing whether Poppet was still anchored in the cove and whether there was anyone at the cottage.

    We carefully made our way, slowly and surely watching the mist lighten as the sun came up. Half an hour later, I guessed we were very close, and whispered to Julie to put the lead on Rusty and stay where she was whilst I took a closer look. I edged my way closer and saw the dark shadow of the cottage looming through the now white swirling mist. It was very quiet and I began to have doubts as to whether there was anyone there. Suddenly, I could see a dark blue SUV parked at the back of the cottage, the same car we saw yesterday. I tried to see if Poppet was visible in the cove, but the mist was still too thick to see anything on the water. I retreated back to Julie, "there's someone at home" I said, "the car's parked there but I can't see the boat. There's a clump of trees close to the back of the cottage which will give us a bit of cover and we should be able to keep an eye on the place without being seen". We made our way quietly along the edge of a hedge, clambered over where it became a little sparse and edged towards a mound protected by trees which would give us a perfect hiding place with a good view, if only the mist would clear a bit. Rusty was good as gold, Julie gave him a drop of water from a plastic bowl she'd brought and I took care of the flask of coffee. We had ourselves a bit of a picnic, perched high above the sea waiting for some movement from the cottage and for the mist to lift.

Chapter 16

More than an hour passed, it was fully light but I still couldn't see whether the boat was still anchored. A noise made both of us jump and I thought Rusty was going to give us away by barking. He growled a deep throaty growl, but Julie spoke quietly in his ear and averted what could have been a disaster. Then, a car door opened and closed, the engine started and the car moved away up the lane. "Show time", I said quietly, "I'm just going to get a little closer to check on the boat and see if there's anyone at home. I crept over the grassy mound to the cottage and peered through the windows listening for any voices or any sounds at all. At the back there was an old outhouse which had originally been the outside toilet, and I saw a cable running from the house to it. The outhouse wasn't locked, I quietly opened the door and found an almost new looking Honda generator. It was cold which meant it had not been used recently. I made my way around the front which seemed to have the only door into the building. Everything remained quiet but I still could not be sure if there was anyone else in the cottage. Although the mist appeared a little less dense, there was still no boat visible, I found the path down to the cove hoping that getting closer would allow me to check out Poppet. I crouched on the beach for what seemed an age watching the mist come and go. Without warning, it swirled and a large clear area developed. Poppet was gone, which hopefully meant that the cottage was empty. I raced back up the path and back to Julie's hiding place. "Where the hell have you been, I was worried sick"? She listened as I told her, "but if the cottage is empty, they may have taken Ricky with them too", she said, a point I had not even contemplated. "Let's hope not", I said, "but we'd better get going before somebody comes back.

We left our hiding place and made our way round to the front door. Again we looked through the windows and listened but there was no noise. "They could still be asleep" she suggested, but we were committed to see this through now and I placed my rucksack on the floor. I tried the door, but it was locked. I retrieved the jemmy from the rucksack and pushed its narrow end in between the door and the frame, opposite the lock. There was some play in the door which helped, I took one final look around and in a single movement, levered the jemmy, and with a loud crack, the rotted wood splintered and the door flew open. We both instinctly ducked, froze to the spot listening for any reaction to the noise we had just made, but there was none, except that somehow Rusty had escaped Julie's grip and was into the cottage before we could grab him.

We both followed into a grubby hallway which lead into an even filthier kitchen. It immediately reminded me of the inside of Poppet, it even smelled the same. There were tools on the kitchen table, some small screwdrivers, long nosed pliers and cutters, a soldering iron and bits of wire on the floor. Julie checked out the small sparsely decorated lounge while I moved slowly into one of the two bedrooms. It was evident that they had both been recently used with a single bed in one, a double and a makeshift camp bed in the other, with clothes left strewn everywhere including the floor. Julie followed in behind me and spotted what looked like a T-shirt that Ricky had worn with a Dartmouth logo on the front which raised our spirits. Behind us, Rusty was sniffing at a bolted door as if he knew there was something of interest inside.

We both looked at each other with some trepidation, what were we going to find in there. I opened both bolts and saw steps leading down into what was obviously a cellar. I flicked the light switch, but nothing happened, so I found the small torch I carried in my jacket pocket and shone it into the darkness. Away in the far corner was a lifeless body covered in a dirty blanket. I slowly descended into the cellar and walked towards the bed, there was a little movement as if someone was cowering away from the light. I edged closer and saw Ricky's almost unrecognisable, badly bruised and swollen face. "Ricky, I called, is that you"? He slowly turned and I could tell he was hurt. It was the first time he'd heard his name since he had been locked up. He couldn't make out who was stood by the bed because the torch had blinded him. "Bobby"? he asked in disbelief. "Yes, it's Julie and I, we've come to take you home". With that, he cried, an uncontrollable howl of a cry of relief as he turned towards me. The blanket slid off his body, which I saw was black and blue, and most of his face was badly swollen with only one eye open. I reached out to him, he was wailing, I tried to comfort him but holding him close sent pain searing through his battered body. Julie came down the steps and when he saw her, with Rusty at her side he let out another pitiful cry from deep inside his soul. He blabbed like a child with relief he thought was never coming.

Julie sat on the bed and gave him a gentle hug. She had never thought to find him so badly beaten and she almost cried herself. "Can you walk Ricky, because I don't fancy carrying you all the way from here"? "I think so" he said, but groaned with pain when he tried to stand. "Just sit on the side of the bed, Julie's brought some clothes for you". She took my clothes out of the rucksack, along with shoes, and the jacket. "You'd better go and stand watch upstairs in case someone comes back" I said, "I'd hate to get trapped in here with Ricky". I gently helped him get dressed, it was almost like dressing a child, he hurt so much, even moving his arms into the shirt sleeves was excruciating. I tied his shoe laces, put his jacket on and helped him onto his feet. "I'm so glad to see you, I didn't think anyone would find me, I'd given up hope", he said. It was difficult to even support his weight to go up the stairs because of the pain, it seemed better for him to walk unaided because he couldn't stand any pressure on his body. I picked up the rucksack and we made it to the top of the steps where Ricky was temporarily blinded by the light. "Where am I" he asked? Julie told him he was no more than two miles as the crow flies from Langham, "then why has it taken so long for anyone to find me"? he said, but just as we were about to explain, we heard the car return behind the cottage.

Judging by where it was parked when we arrived I guessed its occupant or occupants would come round to the door from the right hand side of the cottage. We helped Ricky around to the left side where there were no windows and we waited, keeping hold of Rusty. I took a peep around the corner, there was only one person and he was taking some bags out of the back of the car. I turned to Julie, "when I say, move as quietly and quickly as you can back along the path and try to lose yourself in the mist as soon as you can". "What are you going to do" she asked in a worried voice. "Nothing heroic I assure you, I'll be right behind you". I took another peep just as he closed the boot and thankfully headed for the house the way I'd hoped. "Go go go" I said and watched them reach the path safely. I had the jemmy in my hand and waited for him at the front corner of the house. I heard him approach the door then stop and put the bags down, presumably when he saw the forced entry, but he made no sound. I had the impression he thought we were still in the cottage and made the decision to make my escape while he checked out inside.

No sooner than I had made a run for it, I heard the door crash open and what sounded like angry swearing but in a language I did not recognise. I quickened my pace then ran as if my life depended on it as I heard him turn towards my side of the building. Julie and Ricky had managed to lose themselves in the mist, but fast as I ran, I heard a shout followed by a gunshot which immediately became a searing pain in my left thigh, and I careered to the ground in agony. The man was running towards me as I scrabbled to get up, but he was upon me before I could get no further than onto my knees, he had a vicious grin on his face as he raised his gun to finish me off, but he gave me just enough time to swing the jemmy across his right shin. It was a heavy blow which cracked like a whip and unbalanced him, delaying the shot that would have put all my lights out. I was still struggling to get up when he again swung the gun around in my direction, but out of my right eye I caught a glimpse of a shadow in full flight out of the mist closing on him. Rusty was off the ground and caught him at chest height, bowling him over backwards, and I saw the gun tumble from his hand onto the grass. I made a supreme effort to finish the job and almost fell on top of him as I delivered a crushing blow with the jemmy across his right shoulder. He cried out with the pain but I hadn't finished with him yet. I regained my balance and with all my might, I brought the jemmy down across his left shin which clearly shattered the bone. Rusty was still growling and snapping at his arms, but the fight was over for him, his face was contorted with pain and he lay on his back almost pleading for mercy, which I had no mind to show after seeing what they had done to my friend.

I was bleeding high up on my left leg, my jeans turning crimson but nothing was broken. I hobbled over to the gun and watched my assailant try to back away, but his screams filled the dense mist and all he could do was hold his hands in front of his face as if he expected that was going to protect him. I picked the gun up and aimed it straight at his head, he pleaded for his life, and I just threw the weapon over the cliff edge into the sea and satisfied myself with a severe kick to his already broken leg. Rusty was stood next to me looking proud with his days' work, tail wagging and with all the effort I could muster I made the biggest fuss ever of a dog that had saved my life.

I hobbled away with Rusty at my side and called out for Julie and Ricky who had only been a hundred yards in front of us, crouching behind the hedge. We now had two invalids, Ricky was still very weak and Julie had given him one of the cereal bars and a bottle of water to try and give him a little strength to make it to the car. She supported Ricky while I hobbled along behind, it was slow progress as the path was uneven and undulated. On the flat, both Ricky and I managed quite well, but on any gradient up or down, the pain in my thigh was bad and I was losing a lot of blood. We stopped again and Julie took my fillet knife from its sheath on my belt and cut open my jeans from the bottom up to the top of my thigh. She made light of the two of us, "grown men without an ounce of strength between them" she laughed, and although we were both in some pain, it brought a smile to our faces. She tore the jeans and tied it tightly around the wound to try and stem the flow of blood.

It took a lot longer to walk back to where the coast path met the path up to the Scabbacombe Lane car park. The mist was patchy by now and we could occasionally see the sea down below us. Ricky was still eating cereal bars as he walked, and I limped up the slope. Only about half a mile before the worst was over. We rested, walked, rested again and eventually saw the clump of trees that shielded the car park from the narrow lane. We both struggled over the stile and sat on the grassy bank. I gave Julie the car keys and she walked up the narrow lane to the farm where we had earlier hidden the car. I have never been so relieved to see two car headlights turn into the car park, Julie put my hero, Rusty in the back and helped the two injured warriors into the car before heading back to the safety of Hawley Hall.

While Julie drove, I found my mobile phone in the rucksack and dialled Morgan's number. He answered before it had rung more than once, "we've got Ricky back safely, he's been bashed about a bit, but he's OK other than possibly a couple of broken ribs". "Are you and Julie OK" he asked? "I've been shot in the leg Sir, but Julie's fine, we're on our way back....", he cut me off, "I'll get an ambulance and the Paramedics to Hawley, they shouldn't take long". I was about to ask him how the hell he knew we would be at Hawley, "and we've got some officers on the way to Scabbacombe Cottage too", he interrupted. "How in God's name did you know where we were"? "We have our means Bobby, and what about the kidnappers", "You'll find one of them laid out on the South side of the cottage about a hundred yards along the path, he's got at least one broken leg thanks to Rusty" I said.

Julie was already gunning it down Hawley's long drive which was by now bathed in sunlight, and she skidded to a halt on the gravel outside the stables, just as father and Tim appeared with the Labrador's. Once they had overcome their initial shock, they helped Ricky and I into the big old kitchen, Mrs Harman nearly had kittens when she saw me dripping blood all over her clean slabbed floor, and when her gaze dropped onto Ricky, I thought she was going to faint. "Oh dear me, have you two been fighting"? It took a while for the penny to drop before we all roared with laughter, but it was Ricky who momentarily passed out with the pain from his rib cage.

Mrs Harman had put the kettle on for a nice cup of tea, which all Brits seem to turn to in moments of crises, and boy, didn't it go down well this morning. Father had the first aid box open trying to find a clean dressing to replace the torn jeans around my thigh and stem the blood which was still flowing at an alarming rate. Julie and Tim were trying to make Ricky more comfortable and had moved one of the wooden bench seats from the yard with ample cushions from the hall seats so that he could lay back to ease the pressure on his ribs.

Back up on the coast path, Karin was in agony. He was sure both his legs were broken and his shoulder had a searing pain. He could not move but he managed to find his mobile phone in the pocket of his trousers and he dialled Nina's number. She was already well down the river, almost as far as the higher ferry. She looked at her phone and took the call. Karin was clearly in serious trouble, unable to move and she knew nobody would be able to get to him before the alarm was raised. His final act of defiance was to warn her not to return to the cottage which would be crawling with police in no time.

    She was engrossed in conversation with Karin and took her eye off what she was doing long enough to almost have a disaster of her own. She had sailed Poppet almost down to the town jetty when, out of what remained of the swirling mist came a huge ship whose hull was turning across almost the entire width of the river. The pilot boat, just seeing her in time had fired its horn, and the harbourmaster, who was also out on the river had brought his Rib alongside her hull and was chiding her for not monitoring channel 16 on her VHF. They had picked her echo up on the radar further upriver and had tried to hail her but with no response. If the harbourmaster had not been tied up ensuring the cruise ship was moored safely, he would have insisted that she dock on the jetty for a roasting from the Coast Guard. As it happened, he was so preoccupied with the MS Braemar that Nina and Poppet were able to sail away unchallenged. She rammed the boat's lever fully forward, and although Poppet didn't have a powerful engine, she sped away towards the open sea. Nina made one final call before she threw her mobile overboard, and made a decision to get to safety without any thought to the rest of her team.

The police were all over Karin, and had removed the phone just as he finished his call, taking the mobile away for evidence. Guns were trained on him and he offered no resistance. They tried to move him closer to the road to Scabbacombe but he screamed so loudly they were forced to wait for an ambulance so they could administer some pain relief and apply splints to his legs. The police had already sealed off the cottage awaiting a forensic team, but as there were no witnesses at this isolated spot, were gathered in groups waiting.

Chapter 17

The whole family had gathered in the kitchen by now, and even Brian had come in from the garden to see what the commotion was about. Mother had taken over trying to dress my wound whilst Mrs Harman, with Grandma's help were keeping Ricky comfortable. Julie was by my side looking tired, with Rusty sat obediently with his head on my one good leg. Julie looked pale and exhausted, the realisation of what we had done and the risk we took had suddenly dawned on her and she looked almost as if she was going to pass out. Pippa was the last to appear and she immediately looked after Julie. Father had gone out into the hall at Ricky's request to call Langham and let his family know he was safe. Nathan was also descending the stairs to see what all the noise was, with Amanda following close behind. He had stuck his head around the kitchen door, not keen to witness too much blood and gore before breakfast, but satisfied it wasn't going to put him off his food, he came in, larger than life as usual. "Bit early for a party isn't it, have I missed the excitement"? Amanda was still not dressed, she had come down in the most alluring night gown which barely covered her essential bits, and this, more than any of Mrs Harman's tea had served to miraculously revive Ricky to the point of sitting up, and I thought I spotted his badly swollen eye momentarily open.

Father brought the phone in to Ricky so that his father, Michael could speak to him, just as we heard the first sounds of the ambulance siren. It was the paramedics who arrived first and although Ricky was more badly hurt than I, they were concerned at the amount of blood I was still losing. Ricky had spoken to Elizabeth and his mother briefly and father had taken back the phone so that the paramedics could do their work. I heard him tell Michael that I had been shot and that it was more than likely we would both be taken to Torbay Hospital. They had wanted to ask a lot of questions which father didn't have the answers to, but I heard him reassure them that we would both survive, and had briefly told them that Julie was also pretty shaken up with Rusty having somehow been the hero of the day. One of the medics had moved Ricky on to the floor and was removing his clothing with a sharp pair of scissors so that she could check him over. The ambulance crew were also now checking all manner of vitals, blood pressure, heart beat, and were setting up their stretchers on the kitchen floor in readiness to move us to hospital. It all seemed to take an age but they were so thorough, ensuring that no further damage would be caused by moving us. Julie too was being thoroughly examined and they had determined that she was suffering from delayed shock, but that she had escaped having a hospital visit after Pippa volunteered to look after her at Hawley and take her home when she felt better. Ricky and I were both ready for hospital, the medics insisted that I would remain on the stretcher even though the blood flow from my leg had stopped. Julie knelt beside me and I pulled her down closer, "we did it, you me and Rusty, give him an extra ration of biscuits today and I'll see you later".

The medics had determined that the bullet had gone straight through the side of my thigh and that I needed an x-ray and probably a scan to determine whether any bones or arteries were damaged, and definitely a tetanus shot. Ricky however had some suspected cracked ribs, and they were also concerned with the eye damage as to his sight which had remained blurred. Amanda had ventured close to Ricky and was doing as good a job of caring for him as any medic, but in an entirely different way. They carried us both out to the ambulance and I motioned to Julie that I'd call her, and we were gone.

Morgan was 'marshalling his troops' up at Scabbacombe, but it was the forensic officers from Exeter who had the greater work to do. An ambulance had taken the injured man to hospital and an officer had accompanied him. He had refused to answer any questions or give his name to Morgan. He would have to wait until the forensic team came up with anything from fingerprint or DNA evidence at the cottage. Morgan called Bobby's mobile but had no reply. He had then managed to speak to father who had filled him in on Bobby and Ricky's injuries, but he had also had a brief word with Julie, praising her for her courage. He said he was going on to the hospital himself and that he would 'keep an eye on the boys' for her.

The hospital staff had allowed Morgan to see me, but both Ricky and the 'villain', as Morgan had called him were still in x-ray and it was likely they would both need surgery. I had been given the all clear, it was a deep flesh wound with no further tissue damage, and once I had been stitched up, they expected to allow me home. Morgan dearly wanted to have a right old go at me, but resisted the temptation; he secretly admired our courage but was not willing to say as much. "Tell me Bobby, why in heavens name did you do this alone"? "I don't really know Sir, we just had a hunch, but had no proof of anything. I had seen Poppet in the river and......" "Who the hell is Poppet" he asked, "and for Gods' sake call me Morgan". "Not who Sir, but what, Poppet is a sailboat which I had seen many times on the river and anchored at Scabbacombe, and I just had this gut feel that it had something to do with Ricky's disappearance". "Where's this Poppet now"? Morgan was getting quite agitated. "Why the blazes didn't you mention it earlier". "She wasn't anchored in the cove this morning so I thought no more of her, she's probably on the river somewhere".

Morgan dialled the harbourmaster's number, "Sam, it's Morgan, a sailboat called Poppet with a girl with short black hair at the helm, have you seen her"? It was a longshot, the Friday of Regatta week was the busiest day with boats galore on the river, so it would be a miracle if Sam would remember one insignificant craft. "Saw her this morning, she nearly ran into the side of the Braemar, little devil wouldn't respond to channel 16 so I tore her off a strip". Morgan was getting more and more excited, "you don't happen to know where she is now do you"? "Last I saw of her she was heading out to sea". "Thanks Sam, you're a star". The officers at Scabbacombe had told Morgan that the villain had been talking on his mobile when they caught him." I expect he was warning someone that the game was up which is why the boat kept away. Do you have any idea where it might have gone Bobby"? "If she's not on the river or in the cove, I reckon she may have made a run for it over to France". "Why France of all places"? I would have told him the story about following her a few nights past but thought it would waste time. "If you could get a fast boat out of

Dartmouth on a heading of 143 degrees, I think you'll catch her". "Another of your hunches Bobby"? "More of an educated guess this time Morgan"!

He dialled another number, "Sergeant, is the police chopper available? Good, I've got a mission for you". He explained what he wanted and hung up. "I hope your hunch is right Bobby they'll have my guts for garters if I send that expensive piece of kit on a wild goose chase". Ricky was back, he looked a lot more like his old self, "Nothing broken" he said, just a couple of cracked ribs and some bad bruising, but they want to keep me in overnight for observation, bad luck that, I'd hoped to take your Amanda to dinner tonight, she took quite a shining to me I think". Morgan and I looked at each other in disbelief, he's just taken a severe beating, he's blind in one eye, he's weak as a kitten and the first thing he thinks about is a bit of skirt. "You're unbelievable Ricky, it was a young lady that got you into this trouble, have you not learnt anything"? He just gave us a mischievous smile. "Your friend's not as lucky.....", "he's no friend of ours" we all said almost simultaneously", the doctor had just walked into the cubicle, "well he's got two broken legs, and a shattered shoulder blade, someone gave him a right old beating". "Good on yer Bobby, that's a more fitting justice than the courts will deliver, especially if it ever gets to the European Court of Human Rights, who'll probably release him on the basis he's entitled to a family life to look after his ageing cat! It's a pity you didn't throw the bugger off the cliff Bobby, but don't quote me". Ricky and I looked at each other in shock, and I supposed he was right, Morgan was an old fashioned cop after all! Unbeknown to either of them, Morgan had picked up both their empty plastic coffee cups so that he could use their fingerprints and DNA for elimination purposes. He may be old fashioned, but he was also a clever copper!

Chapter 18

There was utter relief over at Langham, Ellen, who had been beside herself with worry an hour earlier at breakfast, was now excitedly getting ready to go to the hospital. Michael had called George at the plant, who had given one loud 'whoopee' over the phone which had nearly burst Michael's ear drum. The Earl and Ted were visibly relieved having feared the worst as the hours ticked away. Elizabeth was crying tears of joy as she stepped into the back of the Bentley with Ellen, and Michael drove them to Torbay Hospital.

One member of the household, however was less than happy and was fuming at the sheer incompetence of her team let alone the loss of a massive payday for the organisation. She had risked breaking her cover to check who was still active by calling Nina and received no answer, her phone was off. Mo had answered his phone and she was relieved that at least one phase of the operation was still intact. She warned him not to go back to Scabbacombe, to dump the car and acquire another. The conversation was brief and he was instructed to destroy the SIM card and change it to the other one in his possession. Her biggest shock had come when Karin's phone was answered by a voice she didn't know. She hung up immediately, destroyed her own SIM and carried on with her duties.

Mo was already delivering his third load of cider apples to the mill, but he now made a detour via Kirkham Wood to pick up the small thirty litre oak cider barrel which had a wooden plug carefully marked with a cross. He safely stowed it out of sight and drove the tractor to empty his load into the hopper, but called via the stock room to add his barrel to the consignment he was delivering to the house later in the day. Job done, he joined his co-workers who were already enjoying their mid-morning break.

At Hawley, Julie was back to her normal self, both her and Pippa had burst into rapturous laughter at Julie's tale of the tug of war debacle the day before and how Morgan had been pulled head first along the grass. She had also confided in Pippa that she had always been in love with Bobby, as far back as their school days, but that he only had eyes for Elizabeth, until now, and she was so happy that they were getting closer each day. Rusty had also been treated like royalty since returning, with the whole family making such a fuss of him. Mrs Harman gave him treats every time he appeared in the kitchen and Julie thought she should take him home before he was sick. Pippa borrowed Bobby's car and with Rusty safely in the back, headed across the river. Julie's phone rang, it was Bobby, and although Pippa didn't hear all of the conversation, she knew it was good news. "He's OK, they said that it was a deep flesh wound but no other damage. They've cleaned him up, stitched the wound and he's waiting for the doctor to give him the all clear to leave in the next hour. Ricky's not as bad as we thought, but because he's dehydrated and his vision is still a bit blurred, they're keeping him in overnight. Julie was pleased as punch that Bobby was coming home sooner and she was already scheming as to how they could spend some relaxing time together. "I'm going to write up my story now Ricky's safe and hopefully it will make tomorrow's paper, and if I'm really lucky, one or two of the nationals might take it on". "Take it easy", Pippa said, "you've had a harrowing couple of days, I expect Bobby will want to catch up with you later".

Julie's dad was in the shop, "you've got a grin like a Cheshire cat" he said when she walked in the door. She was rather pleased with herself. "Come on then, out with it, what have you been up to, as if I didn't know"? "Whatever do you mean, dad"? "You've had that silly grin on your face since that Bobby's been hanging around, so I'm guessing it has something to do with him". Charles Fairbrother was nobody's fool, he had retired early as a lecturer at Exeter University when Julie's mum had been taken seriously ill with MS when Julie was only fourteen and her sister Sarah a year younger. He had given up a distinguished career and bought the little second hand bookshop in Dartmouth so he could look after both his wife and daughters. Julie's mum had died less than two years later and Julie herself had studied English and journalism at Exeter, but chose to move back to the town to stay close to her dad, who she doted on whilst Sarah was a Marine Biologist working for the Florida Fish and Wildlife Commission in Naples. She made a cup of tea for the two of them and sat down to tell him the whole story, but a customer disturbed their peace, "you can read the rest in tomorrow's paper dad" she said with a twinkle in her eye as she bounded up the stairs to 'commit her tale to paper'.

Morgan was in a fast cruiser headed out into the English Channel, to team up with the Torbay Lifeboat which had been despatched from Brixham. Police work had suddenly become very exciting in this normally quiet Devon port. The police helicopter had picked up Poppet exactly as Bobby had described but had reported that she seemed abandoned about forty five miles out, right in the middle of the shipping lanes, and that she appeared to be taking on water. They were closing fast on the sailboat and as they drew nearer, they could see she was floundering. The lifeboat was already at the scene and had a man on-board, which was risky as it was obvious Poppet was sinking. Poppet had been abandoned and scuttled, there was no sign of Nina. The lifeboat crew were frantically pumping water out but it was coming in almost as fast.

The crewman on-board eventually reported that he had found the main engine cooling intake pipe had been deliberately cut but that he had found the through hull fitting and turned the valve off. Half an hour later, she was seaworthy again and under tow back to Dartmouth. Morgan was on the radio talking to the helicopter flight crew. They reported that a French fishing trawler had been in the vicinity of Poppet when they had arrived. She was called 'Adele' with a home port of Cherbourg. They had noticed nothing suspicious but had photographed the vessel which was steaming back towards the French coast and was now probably back in French territorial waters. Morgan was furious the helicopter crew had not followed the trawler and sent them to find her again. He was like a terrier once he had his teeth into something and he was not going to let Nina disappear into the ether. He called the station who gave him the telephone number of Cherbourg's police and harbour authority, but despite spending at least fifteen minutes remonstrating with them, they had suddenly 'hidden'behind the language' and given him a right old run-around.

He was angry, Nina was not going to get away with it, his next call was to Langham, and a woman's voice he didn't recognise took his call and put him through to Ted. "Foreign Secretary, my name is DS Morgan", "yes Mr Morgan, Michael has spoken of you, what can I do for you". Morgan knew his request was heavy handed but he was hoping that he might exert some pressure via the French Foreign Minister to send a 'welcoming party' out to meet the French Trawler before she docked. The helicopter had reported back that the 'Amelie' was indeed steaming for Cherbourg and he passed on the latest coordinates. Morgan had done as much as he could for the time being and he hoped that Ted's influence would generate some 'entente cordiale'.

The Lifeboat towed Poppet all the way up to Dart Marina where the same forensic team that had earlier been at Scabbacombe would start their investigation.

I was so glad when I saw Tim walk into A&E. Ricky had already been moved onto the ward and I was getting bored. Michael and Elizabeth had come down to see me and were beside themselves with gratitude for finding and rescuing Ricky. They had genuine warmth for what we had done and "would forever be in our debt". Much to my surprise, Ellen had also come in after they had returned to the ward and had embraced me with such feeling, and with tears in her eyes. "I've not been very kind to you at times Bobby, but you are a real friend, welcome at the house, both you and Julie any time you like".

She left just as my brother walked in through the door. "Hi Tim, am I glad to see you, I thought I was going to be stuck here all day". Tim had come straight from a short sea trip in the Blue Dart 120 with a client both father and him were certain would place an order. "When we were coming back into the Dart, the Lifeboat was towing Poppet in with Morgan following in another boat" he said. "Did you see a short haired girl with him" I asked? Tim hadn't seen anybody but then, as he said, he wasn't looking that hard. I hobbled out to the car park, supported by a crutch they had insisted I used for the next couple of days, with strict instructions that I was not to put too much weight on my leg and to attend the local hospital in Dartmouth to have the dressing changed tomorrow morning.

We arrived back at Hawley just after lunch but Mrs Harman had thought I might be hungry and prepared broth for me, "to help you get your strength back, Bobby" she had said. She was a treasure, a real old fashioned type with a heart of gold. I kissed her on both cheeks which made her blush. In truth, I could have eaten a large juicy steak and chips I was so hungry, so I made up for it with an enormous piece of cheesecake for after's.

I hobbled out onto the terrace where mother and grandma were having a natter. They hadn't heard me coming even though my crutch squeaked with every step. "The Earl's doing what" I said having eavesdropped on part of their conversation. "It's rude to listen to other people's conversation Bobby, besides it's none of your business". She wasn't cross, just secretive, "I thought I heard you say the Earl was getting married", I said? "Just shows you how wrong you can be when you eavesdrop Bobby, she said the Earl was 'worried' about Ricky of course". Something was up but they were clearly not going to tell me so I walked down the garden and called Julie.

"Hi Bobby, been thinking about you whilst I've been putting the story together. Just finished, how about we meet up and watch the Red Arrows together later". "Why don't you come over to the marina now" I said, "it's the illuminated river procession tonight so I thought we could dress Pilgrim up together, or what I really meant was that you could do all the hard work while I supervise owing to my bad leg and all"! "How long are you planning on using that old cherry Bobby Hawley"? "I'll supply the lights if you'll haul them up the masts for me, how does that sound"? "Be there in half an hour", and she hung up. I retrieved the box of illuminations from the store shed and used the buggy to get down to the marina.

Dave and a bunch of the yard workers were having their lunch break perched over the dock wall when I turned up. "You're a bit of a dark horse Bobby", shouted Dave, so loud that everyone on the marina heard, " bit of a James Bond I reckon, with a beautiful woman as your sidekick, hope the lovely Julie isn't as badly beaten up as you are". I sauntered over to them on my one good leg, "you old boy's having a bit of a laugh at my expense are you, Julie's fine but Ricky's out of commission for a while, so you're safe to let your daughters and girlfriends out alone, at least for a day or two" I replied!

Julie's car pulled up into the car park and the boys gave her a loud cheer and some raunçhy whistles as she came towards us. They all stood up and clapped when she came onto the boardwalk but their greatest cheer was reserved for Rusty who was given a treat from each of their lunch boxes. Julie was smiling and looking fabulous, "don't give him too much, he's done nothing but eat junk all morning" she said. "Come on then 'Hop Along' where's these lights you want me to fit"? We picked up the box from the buggy and I could feel eight pairs of eyes burning into our backs, mainly Julie's, as we walked down the pontoon to Pilgrim. "First things first, I think we both deserve a cold beer, this being a hero lark is thirsty work"!

Installing the lights was pretty easy as they had been fitted every year for the Illuminated Procession. Once we'd lowered the Genoa, we hauled the first set up to the top of the main mast and secured the other end to the pulpit rail, I unclipped the mainsail and we hauled the second set to the top with the halyard and pulled the bulbs taut to the end of the boom. We did the same with the mizzen mast and I left Julie to run lights around the pulpit, both starboard and port rails and across the transom. I was busy connecting them up when I spotted the 'Magie Noire' gracefully sailing up towards us. She was still a boat that sent shivers up your back and with the French Tricolour flying majestically from her aft rail, she was a very special vessel. Julie was up near the pulpit mesmerised by her elegance and I took her the binoculars just as she was coming about to pick up a buoy South of Sand Quay. Julie spotted a very attractive young lady on deck but teased me and refused to give me the binoculars for a closer look. She had her back to me, I put my arms around her, gently kissed her neck and whispered, "why would I want to look when I'm already with the most beautiful girl in Dartmouth"? She turned around, gave me one of her most alluring smiles and a peck on the cheek, "come along Bobby, we've still got work to do".

We tested the lights which would look stunning when the sun went down. I had earlier phoned Smugglers Landing and ordered some drinks and buffet food for this evening which one of the staff was delivering in one of the marina trolleys. Julie duly stored them away in the large galley fridge, nicking one or two when she thought I wasn't looking in the process, "you've got enough food here to feed an army, how many are we entertaining this evening" she asked. "Including your dad, about twenty". She looked at me in amazement, "dad won't get on a boat", "he's already accepted my invitation, water taxi's picking him up at six along with several of our friends". "You hungry" I called out, "I wasn't, but seeing those lovely morsels have made me realise that we'd not had much to eat today". Pilgrim was shipshape and ready for our evening guests, so we went for a snack over at Smugglers Landing.

Chapter 19

Morgan was still busy with Poppet, the forensic team had finished and he had demanded an urgent analysis of the evidence. He had taken Ricky's statement earlier at the hospital and knew that three people had been involved in his kidnapping. They had one in custody, be it under armed guard in the hospital, Nina, or whoever she really was had seemingly done a bunk, but who was the third person, who according to Ricky was another man. Bobby's statement had not provided any real clues except that Poppet had been seen several times on the river. Where had she been and what were those on board up to? His phone rang, "we have some initial conclusions for you DS Morgan, we found evidence of five different people on board, one of the DNA samples matches your captive at Scabbacombe but we haven't been able to run it through the computer in Hendon for identification yet, there are two others who are also unknown, the fourth one is Richard Gilbert, and here's one which will please you, the fifth one is your victim, Hannah Parker". "Thank you, but please give the highest priority in identifying those three, there's something going down here and I want to get to the bottom of it".

Morgan now knew that Hannah had possibly been killed or at least her body disposed of from Poppet and that it was certain that Ricky had been abducted in Poppet too. Time was ticking and he needed a quick breakthrough if he was going to capture the others. Nina was probably in France, but despite having passed the information and the pictures of the trawler to the French authorities, they hadn't seemed too keen to act on it, and he'd heard nothing back following his conversation with Ted either which frustrated him.

There was a Sea King Helicopter belonging to 771 Squadron out of RAF Culdrose in Cornwall hovering over the river as part of their sea rescue display in conjunction with the inshore lifeboat. Their task was to rescue a person in difficulty anywhere around the South West Coast and they always gave a good show at the Regatta. There was also a party barge running down river with loud music and youngsters jigging and frolicking on deck. It was clear the drink was flowing even this early in the day, and Morgan was enjoying watching their antics, when a large man staggered to the rail, stumbled and was tipped unceremoniously into the water. The crowd on the riverbank cheered enthusiastically at the authentic 'dive' thinking it was part of the rescue display. Neither the helicopter nor the lifeboat made any move towards the man who was now struggling to stay afloat and thrashing in a panic. It wasn't until the party boat captain, who had seen the man overboard incident called for help on the boat's VHF on emergency channel 16 that it was realised this was not part of the demonstration. Within minutes, the Sea King crew had a man in the water, and the lifeboat was rushing to the scene. The Sea King was lowering a harness into the water but the big fellow was fighting the crew member in the water and was in a state of panic. The whole of the rescue attempt was being commentated over the tannoy system, and on the quay a short distance from Morgan, there was further panic as another rather rotund man was threatening to climb over the rail. The whole scene almost became a pantomime with many of the "audience" still unaware that this was no drill. Eventually, the professionals brought the situation under control and Oliver was unceremoniously bundled aboard the lifeboat.

Nathan and Margaret had been in a state of panic until one of Morgan's officers had calmed them down and taken them to the jetty where an ambulance crew were already tending to Oliver, who was out of his wet clothes and wrapped in a thermal blanket. "That bloody family's becoming a liability", Morgan laughed when the officer told him it was a member of the Hawley clan. "I shall rib that Bobby rotten when I see him later".

Crowds were gathering all along the embankment and high on Jawbones Hill as well as a myriad boats on the river in readiness for one of the highlights of Regatta week, the Red Arrows display team. A brass band was playing in the bandstand in Royal Avenue Gardens, the street traders were making a roaring trade with Devon's famous vanilla clotted cream ice cream flying off the shelves.

I was readying Pilgrim for a short jaunt out into the river for the best view of the display. Pippa and Amanda were already on board, although I had to insist she removed her high heels to protect the deck's teak planking, Uncle Nathan and Margaret had chickened out after seeing Oliver fall overboard whilst Oliver himself was "sleeping it off". The water taxi had brought Julie's dad and Morgan, Tim and Georgina had brought mother and grandma down from the house and with less on-board than I had catered for we pushed away from the dock and headed for the lower river just as the Lady Elizabeth made her way from Langham with George at the helm. The whole family, with the exception of Ricky were on board including guests who I didn't recognise. They saw Pilgrim and edged their way over to within hailing distance. Ellen, Michael and Elizabeth moved over to the rail and were clearly still emotional following Ricky's rescue, "would the two of you like to come over to dinner on Sunday", they called, "about seven OK"? I looked at Julie who nodded and we both said "love to" almost simultaneously.

Wind was light and the tide was favourable, the weather balmy with a clear blue sky, perfect conditions for the display. We took up position amongst the many boats and ferries, some of which had come from Exmouth, Teignmouth, Torquay and Salcombe. Their first pass caught us all by surprise as they flew in low from the sea a little above the water with a roar which shook Pilgrim's rigging before they rose majestically into the sky with the red, blue and white smoke trailing behind. They were sometimes so low they barely cleared the towering Braemar and its one thousand passengers who were getting a spectacular view as they soared, sometimes so close, their wings appeared to touch. The display ended with a series of loops ending with two of the Hawks making a huge heart shape in the sky with the remaining five Hawks streaking through the middle like cupids arrow.

We slowly made our way back upriver, father was still entertaining on-board the Blue Dart 120, I edged closer with my starboard fenders down and rafted up so that Morgan, Julie and her dad could have a short tour. Morgan was utterly speechless, which was very unusual for him and even Julie was overwhelmed with her opulence. "This is fantastic, better than any house, grand or otherwise, I have ever been in" said Morgan. Julie's face was a picture, I showed them into the main saloon with its extended balconies, the master stateroom, the galley and the dining room. Morgan was fascinated by the technology on the bridge but was agog when he stepped into the engine room with its twin, two and a half thousand horsepower diesels. As we stepped back onto Pilgrim's deck, Morgan grabbed my arm, "if I was to sell my house, could I afford one of those" he asked tongue in cheek? It was Morgan's way of asking how much it cost, and when I told him it was more than "nine very large ones", I thought he was going to fall overboard.

    We made our way back up to the marina, passing the "Magie Noire" en-route, spotting George on deck getting on like a house on fire with an extremely attractive dark haired, heavily tanned young lady. I could feel Julie's eyes burning into my back, spotted Morgan's jaw drop and went over to him, "don't even think about it Morgan, this one's closer to twenty million"! It was of course possible that his jaw dropped at the sight of the young lady, and nothing to do with the yacht!

    As we approached Sand Quay, all manner of boats, small and large were gathering for the procession, some were still installing lights and lanterns as they sailed whilst on-board others, parties were already well underway. Later, the whole river would be one big party, a nightmare in the making for the harbourmaster, coastguard and lifeboat crews, although if all went ahead without incident, they also joined the festivities.

Pilgrim's party was in full swing, the wine was flowing and the ample food was welcome with a little chill in the air now the sun had gone down. Julie had disappeared into the aft stateroom and emerged wearing a lovely cream pair of chinos with a blue and white striped cashmere sweater finished with a cream Channel silk scarf around her neck. Father brought three of his golfing pals on board and I spotted Dave, our dock master on his way home and pushed a cold beer into his hand, persuading him to join us. I went below, found the CD of 'The Fisherman's Friends", a Port Isaac sea shanty group and their 'Haul Away Joe' was soon coming through the cockpit speakers as we pushed away and joined in at the end of the illuminated procession which slowly sailed away down the river.

Although the crowds of earlier had thinned out, there were still scores of people on the embankment and when the procession turned around just below the Castle steps, we had the pleasure of seeing all the other boats in all their illuminated glory. The 'Fleet' started dispersing on the return trip upriver and we were back on the dock before a light drizzle dampened down the party with a slightly chill wind to send us below. The 'oldies' made their excuses and left taking Amanda with them, Morgan said he'd better get home 'before the missus sends out a search party' and Dave joined him and Julie's dad in the water taxi heading back to town. In less than ten minutes, our little party had disbanded leaving Julie and I still admiring our lightshow before retreating into the warmth of the cabin.

The 'Fisherman's Friends' had been replaced with a little smooth jazz as I poured the two of us another glass of wine and cozied up on the saloon settee. We talked about a day neither of us would forget in a hurry, a day on which we had risked our lives for a friend, found a new hero in Rusty, who was curled up on the saloon rug and whose ears were twitching in full knowledge we were talking about him. A day on which we had done what we both loved, just messing around on the river with our friends and family in a boat, but most of all, a day in which our relationship had blossomed from friendship to an intimacy of thought and touch, a meeting of eyes and soul, a bond of love that was not manifest a mere twenty four hours before.

I leant over to touch her face which had a tenderness reflected in the cosy light of the boat. She smiled, her eyes seemed to have a sparkle I had not seen before, a warmth coursed through my body. We kissed, passionately but tenderly, my hand caressed her neck which seemed to awaken a deep need within her, my lips moved to the crease of her soft neck, there was an involuntary intake of breath as she grasped my hand and squeezed it gently as her desire grew. My hand moved slowly to her breast as she demanded my lips return to hers. We explored the moist sweet taste of wine, our tongues moving like the gentle lap of water on the shore as my hand slipped underneath her sweater to find her firm breast bare, and her nipple hard with desire. She took her hand from mine and worked her way from my chest to my thigh, sending ripples of pleasure through my entire being. I caressed her breast with soft lips as my hand moved from her knee on a teasing line to the heart of her love as she found the same pleasure in descending to my hard and eager manhood. Her chinos released easily as I explored her writhing body, slipping underneath her panties and into her 'garden of Eden'. She arched her back as she hunted for the source of my pleasure, discarding anything in the way to caress my sensile erection, driving it to even greater heights as my fingers fell into her valley of desire, to be met by a torrent of aqueous and dewy warmth, coupled with an imploring moan, I wanted her so badly, we became as one as I entered her moist, tropical chasm and thrust rhythmically to the sound of the clanking halyard brought to life by the gently rocking boat. We were both at the peak of desire when in one symphonic climax, our bodies still entwined in erotic passion, we erupted together into an explosion of pleasure and fell into each other's arms. "I love you Julie, I guess I've always loved you but never saw what is now so clear". "I've always loved you Bobby, I've never had any doubts, I've just had to be patient until you felt it too". The cabin had a sort of quiet contentment about it, the wind playing a gentle tune in the rigging, Rusty's regular breathing and the odd twitch of his wet nose, the gentle rocking of the boat and the soothing splash of water against the hull. This was peace, this was contentment made possible through the love of a beautiful woman. I was so very lucky, I had never appreciated life as much as I did at this moment, and I was looking forward to a whole lifetime of such pleasure with Julie. I walked into the aft stateroom where she was already in bed, and the pleasure continued!

Chapter 20

Everyone at Langham was up with the sun, it was a big day. The house and garden was a hive of activity, deliveries arriving, preening and cleaning from top to bottom, grass having its final trim, a lick of paint here and there, garlands of fresh flowers adorning every nook and cranny, wine from Langham's vineyard was being unloaded from one of the estate vans along with cider barrels from the mill, and staff were hurrying everywhere about their business. Security was also tight with the PM arriving in a few hours.

Elizabeth was already on her way to Totnes to meet her intended, Anthony, who was arriving on the first train out of Paddington. As she stepped onto the platform, she spotted Pippa, stood there seemingly awaiting the same train. "Fancy bumping into you here this morning, we're not both meeting our boyfriends off the same train are we" she asked? The train was late as usual so they stepped into the little cafe on the platform for a coffee, excitedly chatting about how today would be a special day with Ricky coming home from hospital and the arrival of the Prime Minister and her family. "The Prime Minister" asked Pippa? "Oops, I shouldn't have said anything, but today of all days, no secret is safe with me". "Don't worry, I shan't breathe a word, but what an honour, I assume she'll be at the Regatta Ball tonight"? "Oh yes, they're arriving around lunchtime and going for a walkabout down town this afternoon".

The station announcer heralded the arrival of the six thirty out of Paddington and both Anthony, Elizabeth's intended and David emerged out of the same carriage door as if they had been lifelong friends. Both men were in their early forties, dressed in almost matching suits, looking more like city bankers than a diplomat and a musician. The girls were beside themselves with excitement and hurried to meet their respective men. Introductions were almost unnecessary as the men had struck up a conversation on the train and already knew almost everything about each other and their partners.

Ricky was also looking forward to going home having been officially discharged by the doctor an hour earlier. He was still very sore and although his eye was still swollen, the blurriness had gone away. He had been given some painkillers and told to take it easy for a couple of weeks while the bones healed together. The worst advice Ricky had been given was not to drink whilst he was taking the medication so he had elected to not take any pills so that he could still have a drink or two at tonight's ball. He sat in the waiting room willing George to arrive, impatient as he always was to get back to Langham.

Julie and I had removed the illuminations from Pilgrim's rigging and they were packed away safely for next year and the sails hosted back into their proper position. Pilgrim was back to her pristine condition in and out.

I took Julie and Rusty home in the tender as I had a few clients to demonstrate the Regatta 65 to. I dropped her at the town dock and turned the tender towards the middle of the river. I hadn't gone very far when I heard Julie calling from the Quay and excitedly shaking and pointing at a newspaper. I turned around and went back to the dock, she ran down to meet me loaded with four newspapers, the story was on the front page of the local Dartmouth Breeze and also front page in The Daily Express. It had made page three in The Daily Mail and not an insignificant double column in The Times. The headline "Foreign Secretary's Nephew kidnapped and rescued in dramatic cliff top shooting" had certainly made an impact and as we thumbed through the pages, we spotted some news vans setting up around the inner harbour.

Morgan was on the prowl and his eagle eye saw us crouched at the dock. "Oh Oh, we're in trouble again, angry looking policeman approaching" I said, but much to our surprise he was in a great mood when he crouched down beside us. "Great news, I've just heard that Nina is in custody in Cherbourg". Apparently, his various high level phone calls had elicited some action and a heavily armed French Coastguard vessel had stopped 'Adele' outside the Port of Cherbourg, searched the vessel and apprehended her parading as a member of the crew, impounded the trawler and arrested all its other crewmembers. "Great result" he kept saying, "now we've just got to get her back here for interrogation; oh, and I nearly forgot, we've had some DNA results back and the body you found Bobby is a local woman named Hannah Parker from Paignton, and get this, she was either killed or most probably disposed of from Poppet, so there was a connection with Ricky's kidnapping". It was the happiest we'd seen him, "and there was us thinking you'd be mad with us for the newspaper coverage and the TV Vans and everything". He gave a loud belly laugh, "those vans aren't here for you two or Ricky, the PM's in town today, didn't you know, so we're all on 'Nanny' duty for the rest of the afternoon. See you guys later, keep out of trouble"! "Wow, the town is getting some publicity at the moment, can't hurt even if some of it is not all that favourable" Julie said. "Must dash, I've got a potential customer arriving in ten minutes and I need to change first". Julie leaned down, gave me a cheeky kiss and skipped up the ramp whilst I pushed away and headed towards the boat.

Elizabeth arrived back at Langham just a few minutes before Ricky, the family were still in the Great Hall meeting Anthony when he bounded in with George behind. "I'm home", he called, "this is a very formal homecoming for the black sheep of the family"! Elizabeth rushed over and gave her little brother such a hug, he stiffened from the shot of pain, "I'm so sorry Ricky, I forgot you were still hurting", "I'm OK sis, tough as old boots, but it's so nice you've all missed me". They moved into the drawing room where some drinks had been set out for all the guests arriving this morning.

The Earl hadn't surfaced, but Michael and Ellen were fussing over their future son in law whilst Ted, who already knew Anthony, and had in fact introduced him to Elizabeth were chatting to Ricky. Michael formally welcomed Anthony to Langham and hoped he'd enjoy his first visit to Devon. "As you know" he said, "were expecting the PM and her family any minute so we shall be serving lunch in their honour when they've settled in. The PM wants to spend some time in Dartmouth on a bit of a walkabout, so we've arranged to make the journey on the river in the Lady Elizabeth. You're all welcome to join us". Ricky was trapped between Uncle Ted and Anthony but escaped when the conversation turned to politics. He was sure that this was going to turn into a 'heavy' afternoon but he didn't think he'd be able to escape this time.

They could hear a flurry of activity outside as the 'cavalcade' descended on Langham. Elizabeth ferreted Anthony away to their room and unbeknown to anyone, Ricky disappeared through the French doors into the garden. The Rt. Hon Jessica Williams was a larger than life character who dominated the predominately men in her cabinet with a mixture of wit and self-assuredness of a person who knew the answers before the question was asked. Her advisors kept her abreast of the important matters of state, and it was said that she had gathered a fair amount of dirt on each cabinet member, which she had no compunction in using if they showed any signs of stepping out of line. Having said that, she was also a very jolly and likeable person, who was very approachable, and she greeted Ted as if he was an old friend with an embrace which would embarrass most men, but Tom, her husband, and rugged Cornishman was an imposing character himself, a self-made millionaire whose fortune was carved out of the mining industry. Ted introduced the PM to Michael and Ellen, and she brushed away any formalities, insisting they call her Jessica, and she in turn introduced Tom and their children Harry and Sophie. "We're on holiday", she exclaimed, "so no pomp and circumstance please, treat us as you would family or friends", and with that they relaxed with some eagerly needed refreshments before being shown into the guest suite.

Ricky found George walking back from the dock having checked out the Lady Elizabeth. They both stuck their heads into the marquee and were amazed at how opulently decorated it was, the smell of fresh flowers was overwhelming, and the whole Red, Blue and White theme conveyed a very patriotic scene. "Some shindig in here tonight George, who have you bribed to spend the evening with you then" Ricky joked. "You cheeky little sod, if you must know, I have invited the daughter of the French Foreign Minister, Nicole Dubois, and I guarantee you that both your eyeballs will drop straight out of their sockets when you see her, so put that in your pipe and smoke it little brother"! "Sorry I asked, but if she's that pretty, what the hell is she doing with you"? If George could have found something heavy to throw he would have collard Ricky with it. "I suppose you haven't been down the pub yet so your partner doesn't know who she is yet", it was George's turn to tease. "As a matter of fact, I have a most gorgeous eighteen year old lady, a city banker's daughter named Amanda no less, just begging for it, so you will also be ga ga when you lay eyes on her big brother". "Have you met Elizabeth's fiancé yet", Ricky asked. "No, I assume he's arrived by now, what's he like"? "I don't know if

I should comment having just met him for five minutes, but he's way too old for her, he's in his forties for God's sake, and boring too, just like Uncle Ted, I don't have a clue what Elizabeth sees in him"? "Maybe he's got a big c...", George checked himself just in time as Elizabeth and Anthony walked in. "Hi you two, George, this is Anthony, Anthony meet my big brother, George". "Pleased to meet you", they both said simultaneously and George laughed, making Elizabeth give him a strange, 'what was all that about' look? George was still chuckling under his breath which set Ricky off. Elizabeth wasn't sure whether to be cross with them or not, but she thought them both rude. "You two been at the jungle juice already" she asked, "I hope you'll behave yourselves better at lunch, which mummy says will be ready in five minutes", she turned and marched a bewildered Anthony back towards the house. George and Ricky looked at each other and fell about laughing again, "I see what you mean", George said, "he's almost old enough to be her father, what the devil does she see in him"? "Maybe he's..........", and they both had to sit down for fear of rupturing something through laughter. "Stop it for God's sake George, otherwise you'll crack more of my ribs".

They both agreed that lunch would be rather stuffy, so they sneaked down to the FBI in the tender for a quick pint and snack. All his old pals were at the bar and cheered and patted his back at his return.

George wondered whether he'd made a serious mistake agreeing to bring Ricky here, but was rewarded with a sensible response when he suggested they return after they'd eaten and only consumed a beer each. They had time to change before lunch was over in the dining room, and whilst Michael was concerned at their absence from lunch, especially after Elizabeth's flippant comment, he was surprised but happy to find both of them sat on the terrace catching up with a cup of coffee. "Is the Lady Elizabeth ready" Michael asked. "All shipshape dad, are they ready to come aboard"? "Very shortly, they're just freshening up, why don't you meet us at the boat and I'll escort them down.

George gave the boat a final check, as did the officer from the Protection Command of the Metropolitan Police. The PM had elected to walk down to the dock, it was such a lovely day, the birds were singing in the woods and the estate looked a picture in the afternoon sun, Harry and Sophie were enjoying their freedom, running in and out of the trees, until they spotted the boat and raced ahead shouting at their parents to hurry. It was as much as their Nanny could do to keep up with them. They bounded up the gangway onto the deck followed by an out of breath Nanny. Tom surveyed the boat, "she's a beauty" he said, you don't see too many of these this side of the pond. They're a great classic trawler design, but I was surprised to find out recently that they weren't built in America at all, but Singapore". Michael knew this but preferred to keep it to himself. "You certainly know your boats Tom, do you have one of your own"? "I have to confess, I'm a sailboat man with an ageing wooden schooner I keep in Freeport, Bahamas, but Jessica wants me to get something with a few home comforts". "In that case, I'll show you a couple of beauties on the way down, built locally at Sand Quay, the Blue Dart and Regatta range. I'm sure Robert or Bobby would be pleased to show you around".

George had the helm and Ricky and Michael handled the dock lines. They gracefully sailed down towards Greenway and Dittisham with Ted providing the commentary. The river traffic was heavy with it being the last day of the Regatta. Ferries and organised boat trips passed, water taxis hurried from the riverside villages as people gathered for another of the event's highlights, the Battle of Britain Memorial Flight, when the Lancaster bomber is flanked by a Spitfire and Hurricane, flying in formation up The Dart, a sight to behold. Competition was still in full swing in the lower river with crowds flanking both embankments. Union Jacks were on full show and it appeared word had got out that a special visitor was about to descend. Ted had pointed out the 'Magie Noire' to the PM who had extended a wave to the Minister and his daughter who were on deck enjoying the spectacle. Michael pointed out the two blue hulled yachts and it was clear that the 65 foot Regatta had captured their attention. George guided the boat close and spotted me on board. "Any chance of a quick guided tour on the way back", Michael called out? "I'll put the fenders out, just pull alongside" I said, as she turned towards the jetty where Sam had reserved a berth for the Lady Elizabeth to dock.

There were seemingly as many press as there were visitors on the Quay and in no time the PM's entourage had disappeared into the masses. She was a popular Prime Minister who had renewed pride in the country through engineering a recovery of the fragile economy left by the previous government. She was a strong leader who had clawed back power to Westminster that had previously been surrendered to the European Parliament, but had achieved it in a way that had maintained good relations with our neighbours. The feel-good factor was back, and money normally dispersed to the undeserving in the form of overseas aid had been diverted to Britain's infrastructure and armed forces. She was 'walking on air' with popular support at an all-time high. The walkabout had been a surprise but the townsfolk and visitors alike had given the family a real West Country welcome despite a couple of hurriedly put together demonstrations denouncing some marginal government policy. They had watched the competitions on the river, taking sides if one of the teams were 'local'. Of course, it was mandatory for them to sample some local Devon ice cream which the children had devoured, if a little messily!

Pippa had arrived at Hawley with her man having stopped off in Totnes to buy an accessory for her ball gown at one of the many independent clothes shops in town. Mother and Grandma were at home but the men were all on the river. Mother had been taken aback when Pippa introduced David Walton, but had hidden her surprise as a cultured woman would, expressionless, and not revealing her inner thoughts. Grandma had also been courteous but inwardly surprised at the age difference, and although she found him pleasant, she could not quite understand why Pippa was involved with an older, even rather dour man.

They had coffee on the terrace, watching the day's activity on the river. Mrs Harman had been preparing a light lunch for them but Pippa had planned to take David down to town as he had never visited Dartmouth before, there were concerts taking place at various venues and they had planned to listen to a string quartet at St. Petrox Church. "You're going to sit in the church on a beautiful day like this when David has never been to see our fabulous Regatta", Grandma said? "David's idea, he's so into his music and St. Petrox is such a beautiful venue. I expect we'll stroll around Dartmouth this afternoon and watch the last of the rowing events.

Grandma's mobile rang and she hunted through her handbag for an age before she found it, but it had stopped ringing, it was a missed call from Bobby. "How long have you had a mobile phone for" mother asked rather indignantly, "and how is it that Bobby's got your number when I didn't even know you had one"? "Not long", she said, "Bobby showed me how to use it and programmed some important numbers in for me. I've only bought it for emergencies" she fibbed. "Well you'll have to give me your number", just as the phone rang again. "Hello Grandma" I said, it was the first time I'd called her on her new phone, "will you be at home later, I would like your advice on something". "I'll be here until six forty-five Bobby when the limousine will be picking me up for the ball". "OK Grandma, see you later". "What's Bobby up to now" mother asked? "No idea, he wants to ask me something but didn't say what".

I called the marina shop to check if the florist had delivered my order. Jane, the shop assistant answered, "they're lovely Bobby, I've never seen such a lot of beautiful flowers like this before, nobody ever buys me any". "Good, keep them safe Jane, I'll pick them up later, thanks". Julie was next on my list, she was at the hairdresser when I called, "it's simply going to take me hours to get ready for tonight" she'd said. "Shall I pick you up around seven o'clock" I suggested? "Can't wait, must dash, love you Bobby" and she was gone. I assumed that was a yes, and planned what I had to do in the very little time I had left. I was hanging around waiting for the Lady Elizabeth to make her return journey, not sure whether the PM would indeed stop for a looksee.

I needn't have worried, they left the dock and made their way across the river. I lowered the fenders and welcomed them aboard. I could tell that there was a genuine interest, especially from her husband, Tom, whom she'd had to drag away screaming as the time was marching on." I'd love to have seen the 'Blue Dart' if we had more time, but I know Tom won't entertain anything unless it has a mast and sails" she said. Before they'd gone far, I was securing the boat and heading back to Sand Quay myself.

Chapter 21

Grandpa had loved classic wooden boats, and although he had been shrewd enough to move with the times and embrace the move to fibreglass, he loved the smell of polished mahogany and teak, the feel of leather and the look of polished brass. He had bought a classic riverboat after he and Grandma had enjoyed a day out on the Thames during Henley Regatta, more than fifty years ago and brought her back to The Dart to lovingly restore as a birthday present for Grandma Beatrice. Rarely used these days, 'Beatrice' was the perfect boat to take Julie to the Regatta Ball in style, and I was busy arranging a garland of beautiful red and white roses around the cabin top coaming. She looked a picture and with her sliding roof, would provide cosy transport even if the weather was to turn a little chilly later.

I sped up to the hall, I wanted Grandma's advice, mother was the practical one, but for advice on matters of the heart, Grandma was the old romantic who had spurned one eligible bachelor in favour of the other, leaving a grieving heart and a bit of a feud in its wake. I knocked on her door and found her choosing the appropriate jewellery to accompany her ball gown. A stunning diamond necklace had been set aside and although her gown was out of sight, I knew she would be the 'belle of the ball'. "Bobby, come and sit down, can I get you a drink"?

Grandma made a mean Margarita, and I joined her in her sitting room which overlooked the garden and the river beyond. "Let me guess, this is about Julie isn't it"? She was very perceptive too, and I found her easier to talk to about these delicate matters. "As usual, Grandma, you're way ahead of me. Julie and I have only been dating a few days, if you can call it that, but I am totally smitten. I've known her from school but only realised now that she has always been the one." "I've seen the two of you together at the garden party and on the boat last night and you two look like peas in a pod, she never took her eyes off you, so if you're asking me if she loves you, it's obvious she does". "What I'm trying to say is that I already feel I want to make a commitment beyond just dating, even though our love is so young, I already know I want to spend the rest of my life with her and I think she feels the same way". "Your heart will not lie to you Bobby, but are you sure you're not on a rebound from Elizabeth"? She gave me a knowing look, there was no hiding anything from Grandma. "I had an infatuation with

Elizabeth, but I know now that's all it was. It's Julie that's got under my skin and I love her with all my heart. "Bobby, the best advice I can give you is follow your heart, but don't rush it, enjoy each other in every imaginable way, even pledging your true love for her for always, but don't be too eager to walk down the aisle, you're both young enough to just enjoy being together before making a final commitment".

I was disappointed with her advice thinking she would have encouraged me to ask for Julie's hand, but she was also old and wise enough to know the pitfalls; "act in haste, repent at leisure" she had said. I was about to leave when she walked over to her jewellery box, "I'll tell you a little story Bobby, when I was a young whippersnapper, just twenty years of age, my life as a Bishop's daughter had been so sheltered. I was still at college in Exeter and dating two of the most charming, eligible and lovable men in Devon". "Grandma, a two timing Bishop's daughter, I would never have believed it". "There's a lot you don't know Bobby, but in a nutshell, one was a fun loving son of an Earl who liked fast cars and anything that flew, whilst the other was a gentle and loving son of a Lord who loved nothing more than pottering around the river in boats, playing rugby, and he loved his music. That was your Grandfather, James, and one sunny afternoon on the river, he asked me to marry him and the rest is history, but it caused such a stink. I can laugh about it now but it almost caused two young men to drown when they physically fought over me on the dock at Sand Quay". "I guess the other man was William, Earl of Langham"? "Yes, because the day before, we had dinner together and he had bought me a gift"; she carefully unfolded a red velvet cloth and revealed the most exquisite diamond necklace with a single emerald at its centre, "which he placed around my neck and asked me to marry him, taking a matching ring"; she unfolded another identical but smaller cloth revealing a beautiful diamond and emerald engagement ring, "from his pocket to place on my finger. He was on his knee in the middle of the restaurant and I will never forget the look of hurt on his face when I took my hand away and said no. We hardly spoke at all on the way home, I took the necklace off and tried to give them back to him, but he threw them out of the car at me when we arrived back at the Rectory. I cried all night, mainly because of my own behaviour in leading two men on who both loved me, and would have done anything for me. I had no idea that either knew about the other, but the following day, William crossed the river and challenged James and their brawl resulted in both of them nearly drowning". I stood there mesmerised by Grandma's story, visions of the fight between an Earl and a Lord seemed almost surreal, but I could see that it brought a tear to her eyes, more than fifty years later. "Do you think I might be making the same mistake with Elizabeth and Julie Grandma, is that why you told me that story"? "No Bobby, just the ramblings of an old woman who has a chance to make it up to the Earl after all these years, but you'll have to wait until tonight to find out how". She was still looking at the necklace and ring, "I've never worn these since, and the Earl refused to take them back saying he never wanted to see them again". She wrapped them back up and held them out to me, "if you truly love Julie, make her happy and give them to her". "Grandma, I couldn't possibly take these, they hold such a sentimental memory for you". "Bobby, they have only given me pain and regret, but they should be enjoyed by someone instead of hid away in a drawer here, please take them and be happy. Now you must go and let me get ready, it takes a lot longer to put on a face when you're my age you know"! I kissed her on both cheeks, "Grandma, you're a rock, and I love you".

  I left, not realising how the time had marched on, there was activity all over the house with everyone getting into their 'glad rags' for the ball. I was walking on air, excited about the evening and even sang in the shower for the first time I could ever remember. Cars were already arriving on the gravel drive outside the Hall, I peered out of the window and caught a glimpse of Grandma getting into a limo. Doors were banging all over with rumbles on the stairs as the family descended to make their way across the river to Langham.

Father, Mother, Pippa and a man who had his back to me were in the Orangery having drinks, Pippa caught my eye, "where have you been all day Bobby, let me introduce you to David, he's with the BBC Symphony". "Pleased to meet you David, did you enjoy your afternoon at the Regatta"? "We didn't see much of it to be truthful having been to two rather smashing concerts at St. Petrox and St. Saviours". I wasn't sure how to respond to that especially since I caught both Father and Mother raise an eyebrow! "Good, good", I said rather pathetically. "You both look radiant" I said to Mother and Pippa. They did scrub up rather well. "You look well groomed tonight for a change in your Tux, red bowtie and cummerbund"! "Cheeky" I replied to Pippa. "Drink Bobby"? father asked, "make mine a large one" Uncle Nathan boomed, coming in through the door with his entourage in tow. I declined the drink mindful of how little time I had, but caught sight of a very alluringly dressed Amanda as I made my exit. Ricky's one good eye will surely pop out of its socket when he sees her, I thought. Father followed me out the door, "I expect you're going in the launch, saw her covered in roses, what are you up to Bobby Hawley"? "Just want to make it a special night for Julie, we've become rather close of late and where better to make a bit of a fuss of her than at the glitziest show in town". "Good on you Bobby, I'm glad you've moved on from that Elizabeth thing". Father was not too good with words when it came to personal feelings, and I could easily have taken umbrage with his comment, but I was in a good mood and wanted to stay that way. I was just about to say something when more limo's turned up and father sped away to gather "the troops".

I took my car down to the marina and walked down the pontoon towards 'Beatrice'. I was rather pleased with myself, she looked a picture, her wood shining in the late sun. I hope Julie likes it I thought, and a worrying thought crossed my mind; I hoped she wasn't one of those women who were afraid for their hair to be ruffled by the breeze; I kept my fingers crossed.

Chapter 22

I rapped on the apartment door and heard Rusty give a single bark before I heard Julie call, "it's on the latch Bobby, come on up". Rusty was at the bottom of the stairs when I opened the door and it was as much as I could do to make a fuss of him and try and keep his hairs away from my clean, black Tux. Julie was in her bedroom, "almost ready, we're not late are we"? "Loads of time" I lied. I nervously checked my jacket pocket to feel for the necklace and hoped Julie wasn't wearing an old family heirloom.

"Close your eyes Bobby, no peeping". "OK". "Don't open them until I say". "OK". I heard her footsteps come towards me, she paused, "you can open them now". I opened my eyes, my jaw must have dropped, I was speechless, in my wildest dreams I could never have imagined the Julie I saw before me. She wore a cream silk ball gown that followed the contours of her slim body, falling low at the shoulders, revealing just a hint of her shapely breasts, her fiery red hair fell in loose curls about her shoulders and her eyes, oh her eyes, a bright green, almost aqua sparkled almost as bright as her diamond and emerald droplet earrings. Even down to her high heeled cream evening shoes with matching purse, she was perfect and naturally beautiful. I didn't say anything for what seemed an age as I sought the words to describe how I felt at just that moment. "Julie, you are the most beautiful woman I have ever set my eyes on, an apparition of natural beauty, you are lovely, beyond my wildest dreams". I was babbling on as she came closer and hushed my lips before kissing me passionately. "You don't look too bad yourself Bobby Hawley"! "Julie, I have something for you, your turn to close your eyes". I walked around behind her and took the necklace from my jacket and fumbled the catch to put it around her neck. "No peeping", as I guided her towards the mirror, she opened her eyes and looked at my reflection in the mirror. "Oh Bobby, this is beautiful, is it a family heirloom because if it is......". It was my turn to put a finger to her lips. "It is and it isn't" I said, "I'll tell you the story one day". "It's lovely Bobby, and it matches my earrings perfectly, I'll just check my make-up and I'm ready".

"Where have you parked the car Bobby, I don't want to walk too far in these heels"? "One more surprise" as I guided her towards the river. Sam had let me dock 'Beatrice' on the jetty "as long as you're no more than ten minutes Bobby" he had warned. We walked down the slipway and Julie spotted her, "she's lovely, whose boat is that"? then she spotted Grandma's name on the transom, "and those lovely roses, did you do that"? I nodded and stepped into the boat and held a hand out to help Julie aboard.

The river was like a millpond, just a gentle flow as the tide was just ebbing. I was telling her how my Grandfather had bought the river launch after a weekend at Henley fifty years ago as a birthday present. "He was an old romantic and I think you're just like him" she had said. We pottered up the river at a leisurely three or four knots, enjoying the solitude of the early evening. The visitor traffic had all but gone but there were a few small boats making their way to Langham like us, everyone dressed in their finery, all drinking glasses of bubbly or wine and getting into the party mood already. Our champagne was also uncorked, we chinked our glasses together and drank to a heavenly night of revelry.

The dock at Langham was already bursting with an array of small boats, and finding a space was going to be tricky. In the end, I rafted up to the Lady Elizabeth's stern, close enough to the dock to step off safely. We had heard the music as soon as we turned the big bend at Greenway, and now it filled the air with magic. The band had been kept a secret, but we were all assured of a surprise, and now we could hear them clearly, they were indeed a professional group. A fleet of cars were parked on the waterfront to take guests arriving by boat, and within a couple of minutes, we were in the queue awaiting our names to be announced by the Master of Ceremonies, our revered Town Cryer, who needed no PA System to make himself heard above the cackle of excited voices.

I could see father and mother and Tim and Georgina ahead of us. "The Lady Georgina Fowlkes of Compton and The Honourable Timothy Hawley.......... Sir Michael Hawley and the Lady Isabelle Hawley" he announced. There were Mr and Mrs' interspersed with Earl this and that, our Bishop this and Reverend that. We were merely announced as Mr Robert Hawley and Miss Julie Fairbrother, but we were the only couple who received a cheer from the bar area where Ricky was busily trying to untangle Amanda away from Uncle Nathan. It all went quiet after Ricky's cheer, and I believe every head in the marquee turned, with their gazes aimed at Julie, who slightly blushed, and which was followed by a spontaneous applause which took both of us by surprise. We had just made it to the bar when we heard, "The Prime Minister, The Rt. Honourable Jessica Williams and Mr Thomas Williams.......... Lord Michael Gilbert and the Lady Ellen Gilbert.......The Earl of Langham, the Honourable William Gilbert and the Lady Beatrice

Hawley". The room hushed again, semi-shocked at the sight of a 'Gilbert' escorting a 'Hawley' to the Regatta Ball.

The band was hushed whilst the announcements were on and my eye was drawn to the small hoarding carrying their name, 'The Strictly Band, leader Dave Arch' it said. Never, I thought, that was a bit of a coup for the organisers, one of Britain's best known bands from The BBC's Strictly Come Dancing playing at Dartmouth's Regatta Ball. People were milling around with drinks in their hands, looking for their names at the round tables. Michael and Ellen hosted the PM and her Husband, the French Foreign Minister and Ted, whilst the Earl and Grandma humoured the Bishop of Exeter and the Mayor. Julie and I were comfortable seated with 'the youngsters', Ricky and Amanda, George and Nicole and others we knew from the Sailing Club. The band was away again, and what a 'good noise' they made. 'Steppin' out with my baby' was in full swing with many couples already either attempting a Quickstep or just doing their own thing. The cocktails were flowing and there was a buzz as the evening really started to swing.

On the tables were bottles of Devon Spring Water and a selection of warm artesan breads with Devon butter and balsamic vinegar and olive oil. Starters were streaming in from the catering marquee, served by estate and catering staff dressed in white shirts and blouses with full length black aprons tied around their waists, giving a feel of a Mediterranean garden party with all the flowers adorning the marquee. There was Pearl Mozzarella, vine tomato, basil pesto bruschetta, a gazpacho shot dressed with a summer salad, perfect for a warm August evening. Not being an accomplished dancer, I waited for the dance floor to fill before taking Julie for a waltz to 'Mr Bojangles'. 'Love is in the air' was so appropriate to how I felt, that although I had no idea how to dance the Samba, I persevered with Julie pulling and pushing me expertly around the floor.

We had bottles of the local wine from Langham on the table with a selection of Italian Pinot Grigio, Californian White Zinfandel and Chateauneuf-du-Pape Rouge for our French guests. A main course of chicken breast stuffed with locally grown vegetables, shallot and potato rosti, glazed baby carrots and a leek and broad bean salad with a champagne and chive cream was both deliciously presented and tasting. During the main course there was a surprise in store, for not only were the Strictly Band in full flow, four of the show's professional dancers jived around the floor to 'Great Balls of Fire' and were cheered on and on as the performed foxtrots, Rhumba's, Cha Cha's and my favourite, the Argentinian Tango.

Fireworks from the Regatta's Grand Finale were exploding into the clear night sky and many stepped out of the marquee for a breath of air and to watch the show which was clearly visible in the Southern sky. After a dessert of summer pudding, Pimms jelly, macerated strawberries with Devon clotted cream and honeycomb, it was a miracle that anyone had the stomach for more dancing, but numbers like 'I've got you under my skin' and 'Love is all around' ensured the dance floor was heaving, and Julie and I were having the time of our life, deep in each other's world, almost oblivious to the people around us.

The spell was broken with the sound of 'spoon on glass' as The Earl rose to his feet to welcome our distinguished guests and indeed all the people of Dartmouth to Langham. "I have two more special announcements I would like to make: I honour and thank two very special people tonight, who through their unselfish bravery, rescued my Grandson Richard, Ricky to most of you" he chuckled, "I of course mean our neighbours and friends, Bobby Hawley and Julie Fairbrother". The marquee erupted into a cacophony of sound as guests stamped their feet and clapped enthusiastically, which embarrassed both of us in the extreme.

On a more personal note, more than fifty years since I first popped the question, the Lady Beatrice Hawley has finally agreed to marry me". The floor erupted once more and the band gave an impromptu rendering of My Fair Lady's 'Get me to the church on time', which brought the room to raucous laughter, and just as the two 'elders' took to the floor, they somehow seamlessly changed into Frank Sinatra's 'It Had to be You', further embarrassing the octogenarians.

Fun over, the dance floor filled to Abba's 'Dancing Queen', I spied Pippa and David having a heated discussion as she tried to prize him out of his seat to dance. Julie saw what I was looking at, "is that the musician fellow Pippa's seeing" she asked, "he seems far too old for her", "and boring as hell, I briefly spoke to him this evening and he seems to have none of Pippa's love of life, just obsessed with his music". "They're certainly going at it now", and with that, Pippa marched off in quite a huff. We were people watching, and both commented almost together what a lovely happy couple Tim and Georgina were together. "That's the girl off the black yacht with George" she said, "wow, she's pretty in that black dress". I was looking at Julie watching other people, there was nobody as lovely as her, and I wondered why it had taken me so long to realise it. Her eyes met mine, and I felt as if she knew exactly what I was thinking, she smiled and kissed me gently as we swayed to the music.

Ricky looked remarkably well considering his ordeal only ended the day before, and I guessed that the young Amanda had been a real tonic for his spirits, body and soul. Elizabeth on the other hand seemed to be suffering the same fate as Pippa, her fiancé, Anthony had spent the entire evening talking politics to Ted and the Monsieur, Julie remarked that they may just as well have retired to an office, whilst poor Elizabeth looked utterly depressed.

The band changed the pace up a gear so Julie and I headed for another round of drinks at the bar, which by now was three deep. The temperature in the marquee had risen with the heat from more than five hundred gyrating bodies and we stepped out to the terrace for some fresh air. Pippa was stood talking to mother when we joined them, "what do you think of Grandma's news then, she kept that quiet" I said thinking maybe that's what they were talking about. Pippa was clearly unhappy and I had stumbled into 'girlie' talk. Julie also realised that Pippa had been crying and put a comforting arm around her whilst I retreated to the 'little boy's room'.

Morgan was stood at the urinal with his back to me, "so this is where all the big plonkers hang out then" I said, "no room here for little willies" he snapped back smiling. "How's your leg holding up after all that dancing then Bobby, and by the way, your Julie looks absolutely stunning tonight, if I was a year younger I'd give you a run for your money lad". "She does look beautiful doesn't she, there isn't anyone here tonight I'd rather be with, I just love everything about her". "Well you make sure I get an invite to the wedding won't you" he joked. "Talking of women, are you any further forward with connecting Hannah Parker with Ricky's abduction" I asked, just as Ricky appeared. "What was that about me and Hannah" he asked, "definitely not guilty there governor" he chirped. Morgan swung around before he'd finished peeing and almost gave Ricky an unwanted shower. "Christ, careful Morgan, I know you've got a big truncheon, but I don't want to bloody see it"! "What was that about Hannah, you knew her" he urgently asked? "What do you mean knew her" he said, "has she gone somewhere"? Morgan was getting agitated now, "for God's sake Ricky, how do you know Hannah Parker, it's important"? "She's our housekeeper of course" he said, as if everyone should know that. "How long has she been your housekeeper" Morgan asked, getting more and more excitable by the second, and I must admit, I was curious as to how Langham's housekeeper had turned up dead and caught up in Pilgrim's propeller. "I don't know, three or four months" he said, why the hell is she important anyway"? "Is she here tonight" Morgan asked? "Yes, I suppose so......" and before Ricky could say anymore, Morgan was marching him out of the door, "you're going to help me find her, I'll explain on the way, pick up your step lad, this is bloody serious".

My mind was also working overtime, how could a woman who'd turned up dead under my boat still be working at Langham? Morgan and Ricky almost ran back to the marquee, "you're my eyes" Morgan had said, "find your housekeeper for me". They were walking around the inside of the marquee but were constantly interrupted by people wanting to talk to Ricky, forcing Morgan to intervene and drag him away. They went all around the marquee, there was no sign of her. They headed for the house, going through the kitchen which was still busy with catering staff; still nothing.

I was making my way back to the terrace, a thousand thoughts going through my head and not looking where I was going, when I almost crashed into one of the bar staff rolling a barrel of cider into the marquee. "Oops, sorry" I said, but he looked rather sternly at me and grunted his displeasure. I carried on towards the terrace but glanced back as he was lifting what looked like a really heavy weight for a smallish barrel onto a trestle. He saw me glance over and made a point of closing the marquee flap at the back of the bar. Strange man I thought, and just then a light breeze caught the flap, and I saw that the barrel had a small red light just where the tap would normally be fitted. I don't know whether it was his attitude or the light that alerted my suspicions, probably both, coupled with the conversation with Morgan and Ricky earlier, but I just had to take a look.

Ricky and Morgan were back in the marquee on their way to the various other smaller catering and preparation tents alongside. She had somehow disappeared but Ricky was adamant that she was on duty and that he had seen her earlier that evening.

I approached the back of the bar cautiously, something was telling me all was not well, I lifted the flap sheepishly, which turned out to be a small stock area adjacent the bar, but as I turned to look for the barrel, I saw the man knelt, pressing some buttons on what looked like an electronic timer fitted to the barrel. My pulse raced, Jesus, it was a bomb, my first reaction was to shout out a warning which I knew would cause sheer panic, but before I even had time to open my mouth, he had pounced and utterly took my breath away with the force of his attack. He caught me with a perfectly executed kick to my groin and upper leg, sending a spike of searing pain to the left side of my body, I fell to my knees and knew instantly that my wound had reopened. He was coming at me again, and before I managed to get back on my feet, his fist caught me on the side of my temple which almost put my lights out, but he was not finished with me, he was lining up another lethal kick which I knew I was unlikely to survive, when to my own surprise, I fielded, throwing him off balance by finding some inner strength from somewhere to tackle him around his legs, bringing him crashing to the ground. I had to somehow get to that barrel and either disarm it or remove it, but I had no idea how I would achieve either because before I had taken a step he was back, giving me a right old pasting with both his fists. I was no match for him, he was clearly a trained fighter, and I found myself flat on my back yet again. My only hope was to try and dislodge the barrel by knocking it off the trestle somehow, and I realised that the only way I would achieve that was by allowing my assailant to knock me flying towards it, because he was far too fast and accurate for me to pose much of a danger to him. I made it to my feet and managed to place myself between him and the barrel before his assault bent me double, and I was determined to make my legs work me backwards to the barrel before collapsing in a heap.

I crashed backwards, the barrel breaking my fall which was all it needed to career off the trestle and roll away under the flapping canvas of the marquee. His attention was now diverted as he leapt after it, but it was me who now had the upper hand, and I managed to trip him up in his hurry to catch it. He was shouting, "Hannah, Now, Do it Now........Hannah, le faire maintenant". There was urgency in his voice, almost panic, and although I was in severe pain, my leg badly bleeding and running warm down my leg, leaving a dark patch even on my black trousers, I was up before him and managed a kick of my own with my good leg. I spotted the barrel rolling away down the bank to the sloping lawn, gathering pace all the time. "Hannah, Do it Now .....Hannah, le faire maintenant", he was screaming at the top of his voice, which had drawn a fair crowd from the bar, including bar staff, and thankfully for me, two of the PM's protection officers, because he turned and with one viscous blow, knocked me flying before the two of them brought him down.

Meanwhile, his cries had drawn Hannah's attention, who was emerging from the ladies room carrying what looked like a mobile phone, which she was anxiously fumbling with. Morgan and Ricky were just coming out of the marquee near me, "there she is" shouted Ricky, "for God's sake stop her Morgan, that barrel rolling down the lawn is a bomb". I was screaming at him, but it was Julie who put two and two together, spotted who Hannah was from our pointing and screaming, and in one leap, cleared the terrace steps and flattened Hannah when her high heels dug into the grass, trapping her legs and causing her body to crash into Hannah, dislodging the phone from her grasp.

Julie was desperately trying to hold on to her but was taking as severe a beating as I had from my assailant. Instead of helping, the other people on the terrace stood like gawking spectators, frozen to the ground like statues. Morgan was chasing up the lawn as fast as his chubby legs could carry him, with Ricky hard on his heels. Julie was taking such punishment, and whilst I had managed to get up to my feet, I was so weak, it felt as if I was running through a swamp. The barrel continued its journey down the sloping grass, gaining speed all the time towards the river. My eyes were fixed on Julie, she was almost spent, when to my horror, I saw the glint of a blade in Hannah's hand, and with one movement, Julie fell to the ground like a rag doll.

Before Morgan could reach her, Hannah had recovered the phone and with a simple press of a few numbers, had done the unimaginable. The world seemed to switch into slow motion as eyes turned to the barrel careering down the bank to the river. The drivers and security staff at the dock leapt behind their vehicles as the rolling barrel plummeted down the final bank onto the wooden dock and disappeared over the edge into the water. Before anyone could breathe a sigh of relief, it detonated with an ear splitting deep boom, sending a huge water spout hundreds of feet up into the air. Fragments from the explosion smashed into the two cars, their windows blown to smithereens and lifting them onto their sides nearly killing the men sheltering behind them. The lights on the docks went out, but not before the trees were stripped of their leaves on both banks of the river and were falling like confetti. The impact of the blast was felt as a warm but fierce wind which rattled the canvas of the marquee, blowing one of the smaller ones over, along with people who were stood watching the horror unfold.

Our world was in stunned silence, people still frozen to the spot in fright, Morgan and Ricky had been blown clean off their feet and I was teetering like a drunk trying to reach my badly injured Julie. Morgan made it before me, the scene that awaited me was horrific, Julie was lying face down on the lawn with blood staining the grass. It wasn't until I knelt down beside her that the full horror hit me, I slowly turned her over, her beautiful evening gown was turning a bright crimson, her eyes were open but she was in shock, unable to focus. It was then I noticed the knife, the handle protruding from just below her chest where blood was oozing freely. With sheer panic in my voice, "call an ambulance, is there a doctor here, Julie needs a doctor, for God's sake, someone get a doctor". My voice was frantic yet breaking with emotion,

Morgan was on the phone, equally agitated, screaming he needed an ambulance immediately and ordering they put the Devon Air Ambulance in the air. Ricky had raced into the marquee and grabbed the microphone from a stunned band leader," Doctor Jarvis, where are you, doctor Jarvis..."over here" she called, "follow me doctor, Julie's been stabbed". His voice was shaking with emotion. Mother and Pippa raced out of the marquee together and stopped, looking down at the life draining out of Julie. The colour drained out of their faces and I thought mother was going to faint. Pippa knelt by Julie's side and held her hand, she looked at me, tears streaming down my face. I cradled Julie in my arms, doctor Jarvis moved Pippa to one side, she felt for her pulse and looked at her eyes, then the knife, still sticking out of her. "Can't you take that out and stop the bleeding" I begged, knowing that it would likely cause more damage and suffering.

Julie turned her head to me, "I'm cold Bobby, so cold" she whispered. I took my jacket off as did a man stood behind me I didn't know, and placed it over her. Doctor Jarvis called for some blankets and someone rushed off towards the house. She'll be alright won't she doctor" I pleaded, but at that moment in time, I was fearful I already knew the answer. The doctor put a hand on mine, all we can do is keep her comfortable until the ambulance arrives". Tears were streaming down my face as I watched helpless as Julie's life faded away. Ricky was crying like a baby by my side, Julie smiled a half smile and tried to wipe a tear away from my cheek, but she didn't have enough strength to lift her arm. Someone had told Grandma what had happened and she rushed over with my father. The look of shock on her face almost reduced me to a pitiful wail, I was sobbing uncontrollably, almost unable to breathe through grief. I kept telling Julie how much I loved her, which seemed to ease her suffering, but she was lifeless, managing the odd sign of recognition, the sparkle from those beautiful eyes draining away. I reached into my jacket pocket and found the small cloth that contained Grandma's engagement ring. I was shaking as I unfolded the velvet and held the sparkling ring so Julie could see it. "Will you marry me Julie", she smiled, and with almost the last breath in her body, said yes with a weak nod of her head. She closed her eyes, she'd gone, her hand went limp in mine as I slid the ring onto her lifeless finger.

The people around us had managed to keep their composure up until that moment, but like me, broke down and unashamedly and freely cried. I could hear the helicopter approaching, Morgan was guiding it in with his radio, landing on the lawn just beyond the marquee. Two medics jumped out and Morgan pointed to where we lay. The sound of a distant ambulance siren filled the night air as the medics knelt down by Julie's lifeless body. It was too late, all too late, all I could do was watch as they looked at each other, then at me and shook their head. The ambulance crew were also there, but could do nothing but gently lift her limp body onto the stretcher. One of them put the blanket over her face which I pulled back, "don't cover her face, please don't cover her beautiful face" I said as they carried her away from me. If my father had not caught me, I would have collapsed in utter despair.

There were other people injured, mainly from flying debris, but down at the dock, there were three badly hurt from the force of the blast and shattering glass. Two more ambulances arrived as the paramedics worked on my leg which was still bleeding, along with the cuts and abrasions to my face from the beating I'd taken. Luckily, the stitches were mostly intact and they were able to repair the damage without the need for me to go to hospital. I stepped into the ambulance still hoping Julie would open her eyes and smile, but seeing her lifeless body welled me up again, mother comforting me with a shoulder to cry on, which became more of a pitiful sobbing as the ambulance doors were closed and she was taken away from me.

The band were playing again but the soul of the party had been ripped out by what had happened, many were comforting each other, sat at the tables, some clearly in shock being given cups of sweet tea. Police were running in all directions, the PM's protection officers had advised her to retreat to the house but she had steadfastly refused to budge. The French Minister and Nicole had gone but the vast majority of the guests were still trying to salvage the evening.

The air ambulance took off as soon as the other medics had arrived, but the police helicopter was overhead hunting down Hannah, or whoever she was. I became stupidly stubborn and insisted that I was OK to go home in 'Beatrice', not realising that I was in no fit state to do anything of the kind. The only way father and Tim managed to calm me down was when they agreed to take me down to the dock. If it hadn't been a full new moon, we wouldn't have seen the extent of the devastation. One of the two cars was over on its side, all the glass was blown out of its windows and three men were receiving attention in the back of the ambulance. The Lady Elizabeth was severely damaged on her port side with parts of her structure dangling in the water. Two cabin cruisers were sitting on the bottom of the river with their bows up in the air. Smaller boats were half drifting half submerged, but I couldn't see 'Beatrice', as the force of the blast had lifted her onto the bank behind the Lady Elizabeth. I cried again at the sight of red and white roses floating in the dark water amongst branches and leaves from the overhanging trees. There was no dock, just splintered planks of wood strewn everywhere and the odd piling sticking out of the water.

Morgan appeared with two officers who had been searching what was left of the boathouse. I hadn't noticed it, but the sheer force of the explosion had torn the front overhang and dumped it thirty yards downriver, and a large branch had fallen hiding what was left. I was increasingly finding it more difficult to speak as the enormity of what had happened sunk in and the shock took its toll. I heard father ask if they had caught them, but Morgan shook his head, "just the man Bobby tackled but the woman who calls herself Hannah has disappeared into the darkness. The helicopter has thermo-imaging and night vision equipment but has had no trace of her yet. They thought they had picked someone up near the river, but it turned out to be a local poacher. We'll get the bitch even if half the Devon and Cornwall police force has to be dragged from their beds". I said nothing, I could only think of Julie's life taken, and for what? "How's he holding up" Morgan asked? Father and Tim looked at me as I vacantly stared into the black void. "Take him home" he said, "there's no more any of you can do tonight". I needed no persuasion, all of a sudden I felt exhausted, as if life itself had been drained out of me.

      They sat me in the back of the car like a dressmaker's dummy, seemingly unable to think or do for myself. Father and mother sat either side of me and Georgina sat in the front with Tim who drove us home. Within sight of Dartmouth, I tried to insist they took me to Julie's flat so that I could explain to her father what had happened to his lovely daughter. Of course, they would not hear of it, but father did find Morgan's phone number and suggested someone should go round there in case he found out from another do-gooder. "All taken care of" I had heard him say, and I felt myself well up again. I liked Charlie Fairbrother, and the tears rolled down my face as I thought of the pain he would suffer having already lost his wife, and now the daughter he doted on.

We were back at Hawley in no time, mother had called Mrs Harman and she had tea brewed and some sandwiches prepared. I sat at the kitchen table where only a day ago we were congratulating ourselves for finding Ricky. "Why, oh why had we not just let the police handle things, Julie would be alive now" I asked to nobody in particular, but mostly to myself. I drank a little tea and allowed mother to help me up the stairs. She waited, sat on the bed as I washed Julie's blood, and my own from my bruised body, and cried again as I watched her life blood drain away again in the shower. Mother sat with me, neither of us saying much, but it helped as she ran her fingers through my hair, just as she had when I was a little boy, and tonight, I wished I could turn the clock back.

Chapter 23

I had been awake since dawn but didn't have the will to heave myself off the bed. Pilgrim drew me, but I knew she would merely remind me of Julie and the horrors of the previous night. There was a gentle tap on the door and Pippa came in with a tray of tea and toast. "I thought you'd be awake" she said, "so I've brought you some toast and Mrs Harman's homemade marmalade". She put the tray down on the bed, " sit up then, it'll remind you of when we were ill as kids and we were allowed breakfast in bed". I smiled, a half smile, and she leant over and gave me a big hug. It was difficult to avoid the pain of last night but she talked as I nibbled at the toast, telling me how David had been a complete bore and that she had taken him to the station to catch the first train back to London this morning, "good riddance" she said. "He was a bit old for you" I said, feeling a little better after munching the toast.

"We're going to church this morning Bobby, and I want you to come with us" she said. I was already shaking my head, "no, I can't face that today,

God has a lot to answer for, and I'm not minded to listen to how merciful he is when Julie's lying on some cold slab in a mortuary". "I'm no expert" she said, "but when a friend of mine was killed by a drunken driver outside the Guildhall School of Music, my friends persuaded me to go to church with them. I cried throughout the service, but it helped in releasing the grief instead of bottling it up inside". She shed a tear, "I know how much you loved Julie and I know how much she loved you, she was madly in love with you way before you even noticed her". We were both crying again, "I was going to ask her to marry me last night when we were alone in 'Beatrice', on the way home in the moonlight". I know "she said", Julie would have gone to the ends of the world to marry you Bobby, and even with her last breath, I saw her smile and say she would". "But she died before I even put the ring on her finger", I was crying again, "that doesn't matter Bobby, she heard you ask and she said yes, the ring is only a symbol, she loved you with all her heart, she told me only a few days ago". "And she's left me with a broken heart because of my stubbornness, doing things my way and not letting the police do their job". "Who was there at your side, supporting you all the way? Julie, don't beat yourself up, she wanted to be there with you". "Then I killed her, just as if I'd stabbed her with my own hands". "Don't be ridiculous Bobby, you've killed nobody,

Julie and you saved several hundred lives last night, including your entire family, not to mention the PM, the Gilbert's, including your friend Ricky, and a large part of the population of Dartmouth. You should be proud of yourself, and Julie would have wanted nothing more than being able to write about it today. What an epitaph for her, she will never be forgotten". "I'd give my own life to have her here right now, and it's hard to contemplate life without her". "Bobby, you're grieving right now, come with us to church and let your family and friends help you get over this".

We sat quiet for what seemed an age, she was imploring me to do as she asked. I wanted to go and see Julie's father, so I agreed. When I came down, they were all in the sitting room, father and mother, Tim, Pippa and Grandma. I went up and gave Grandma a hug, "sorry I messed up your special night.....", she hushed me. "Bobby, what you and Julie did last night was to allow us to live to enjoy it. Don't you ever think any differently because I know Julie would not thank you for it. Now, us Hawley's are made of stern stuff so let's go and give thanks for her short but full life, and at the same time show these terrorists that they will never break our spirit".

We drove down into town, it was a quiet Sunday morning, Regatta was over for another year, the street market was already cleared away, the river calm with just the odd boat and the ferries moving.

We parked and walked the short distance to St. Saviour's, I stopped at the gate and looked up at its ancient tower, "why is it that God and the Bible is losing the battle with Allah and the Koran" I asked? "Bobby, come along, were already late" father called as he and mother walked up the path to the door. Grandma and Pippa wondered what the hell I was on about. "These Islamist terrorists or Jihadists spread their vicious hatred in our Christian country, and God stands by and does nothing, politicians do nothing, the do-gooders and human rightists tie our hands behind our backs and kick us in the balls, whilst the great British public stand by and let it happen. Grandpa and all those like him who fought in two world wars to defend our freedom must look down on us and scream at us to do something, but we can't or won't hear them. How can I worship a God who does nothing while innocent people like my Julie lies dead at their hands"? I looked at Grandma, I knew she agreed with me but like most people who went about their day to day lives just a accepting the ineffectual self-preserving policies of our politicians, turned the other cheek. "I can't come in, you go in without me". They pleaded with me to let my grief take its natural course in the presence of God, but I was bitter, I wanted an angry God, a God who bared his teeth now and again, a God who fought back and won, through strong leaders and people who said enough is enough. I could not go in and simply praise this merciful God whilst Julie's father grieved for his daughter, I turned around and shook my head and walked to the little bookshop, and a lonely, grief stricken father.

I knocked on the door and Rusty barked, he didn't come to the door, I knocked again, "it's Bobby Mr Fairbrother, please let me in, I need to talk to you". Still nothing, I could hear Rusty sniffing the air at the bottom of the door, " go and get him Rusty, good boy, go". Rusty barked and I heard him run back up the stairs, I have no idea what he did but within a couple of minutes, the door opened and a very dishevelled Charlie Fairbrother appeared, he'd been drinking, who could blame him, but he held out his arms and cried like a baby. I closed the door, helped him back upstairs and cried myself as I saw her picture above the settee in the living room.

He looked terrible, I went in to the kitchen and made us a cup of strong coffee and we sat and talked, and talked, and talked. We spoke of her childhood, he had been looking at a photo album. There were pictures when she was a little girl with her first bike, happy pictures with her mum on Slapton Sands, she was the spitting image of her mum, pictures with her younger sister, Sarah. They spanned her whole life including one standing next to her proud father on her Graduation day at Exeter University. "Would you mind if I borrowed one or two of these pictures, I'll take good care of them and promise to return them in a few days"? He graciously agreed, I looked through them again, but it dawned on me, there would never be one with me, her fiancé. We both broke down when I told him I had proposed to her the night before, and she'd said yes. But there would be no wedding, no grandchildren and no life for us.

Rusty looked lost, he was such an intelligent dog and he knew something was wrong. He had sat with his head on my knee as if he was looking at the pictures with us. Charlie had brightened up considerably as had I, talking about Julie, who we both loved in entirely different ways had helped both of us cope with our grief. I got up to leave, Rusty stood to follow me, I knelt and hugged the old dog who seemed to be hurting as much as both of us. Charlie surprised me, "Bobby" he said, "would you consider looking after Rusty, he was so much Julie's dog and it seems appropriate that you should keep him". I was stunned, I felt sure he would enjoy having Rusty around for companionship, but he asked if I would like to have him as I seemed to love him so much. We embraced again, and although there were tears, we were both stronger after our long talk, I picked up Rusty's bowl and a bag of his favourite food, his lead which was hanging behind the door and left. A cloud had lifted, several more hung about me like a damp fog, but I felt more able to accept life without Julie, but was sure many dark days lay in wait. We walked down to the dock to catch a water taxi back to Sand Quay.

Morgan had been up all night with no sleep, and he had kept his promise, half of Devon and Cornwall police personnel were scouring the countryside searching for Hannah. There were police everywhere, even searching the river in small inflatables, combing the banks and empty buildings just like I had one night looking for Ricky.

Sam stopped me by the embankment and made a right old fuss of Rusty. "How are you holding up Bobby" he asked, "terrible tragedy, Julie was one of us and her life snuffed away by madness and evil, here in little Dartmouth too". Just hearing Julie's name mentioned caused me to well up and Sam put a mate's arm around my shoulder as he knew I couldn't speak. "I know it's no consolation" he said, "but we'll get the bastards that did this, even a couple of my lads are out there looking". I looked out across the river, there was still debris from the explosion floating in the water, with Sam's people clearing the most dangerous flotsam. Down below in a corner of one of the berths was a single red rose floating amongst some leaves. Sam watched me kneel on the pontoon and reach down to pick it out of the water. I cupped it in my hand even though it looked a little bedraggled, and told him the story of what I'd done to 'Beatrice'. He already knew of course but let me tell it all the same. It wasn't until I told him Julie had agreed to marry me just before she died that tears he'd been holding back flowed freely down his face.

A water taxi took Rusty and I back to the marina and Pilgrim. I helped him aboard, opened the hatch and dropped down into the saloon. I knew what to expect when I opened the aft stateroom door, I had intended to make last night very special for Julie and had covered the bed in white and red rose petals. They were undisturbed, a cruel reminder of a night which had started as I had planned but ended in tragedy. I collected each and every petal, found a little oak box in a drawer and saved them.

It was time I changed out of my Sunday best, Rusty and I were going sailing, the wind in my hair would help blow some of the cobwebs away. Rusty had his nose in the air, Julie's scent was everywhere and he was missing her as much as I was. I left a message on my father's voicemail and cast off my lines and headed for open water.

The wind had picked up a little and I was already enjoying the freedom as I passed the town dock. I could see Morgan on the Quay talking to Sam, they saw me and my VHF crackled into life, "Pilgrim, Pilgrim, this is Morgan, over". "Morgan, this is Pilgrim, over". "Switch to channel eight", he said. We spoke briefly, Morgan sounded shattered, he was just checking where I was headed. They hadn't found Hannah and the trail had gone cold, "but we'll get the bitch even if I have to knock on every door and stop every car" he'd said.

Rusty was back in the saloon sniffing under the forward cabin door and whining. He was looking for Julie and clearly pining for her just like any dog would, he could probably smell her, and was confused as to where she was. I knew dogs were more intelligent than owners give them credit, and I believed Rusty loved Julie as much as she loved him. I called him with one of his favourite biscuits in my hand and he came running.

The wind was stronger than I expected out in the bay, at least a force five or six. I raised all the sails and winched them in hard to head as close to the wind as I could. We headed out to sea, Pilgrim was in her element, it kept my mind occupied and dulled the memory of last night.

Rusty was back at the forward cabin door, I switched the helm to autopilot and went down below. "OK Rusty, let's satisfy your curiosity, Julie's not here". I opened the door and was faced with a pistol aimed at my head. Rusty raced in barking and growling, "call that dog off or it will join its owner, dead". Hannah's icy cold eyes stared at me, there was a smirk on her face which tormented and willed me to strike at her. I called Rusty to heel and like the good dog he was, he obeyed. "Don't even think about it Bobby, you'll be dead before you make one step". It was as if she was reading my mind. "Back off and take that dog with you". I did as I was told thinking all the time what I could do to disarm her. "Back up, back, both of you into the cockpit, now". I had no choice, Rusty went ahead of me and I made him sit in the cockpit well. She climbed up half way and stopped, out of sight of any boats that may have been out in Start Bay. "We're all going on a little trip" she said, "you're going to take me to France, and if you're a good boy, I might let you live". There was real evil in her voice, she was someone who enjoyed killing, I would need to be very careful not to antagonise her, but I was under no illusion that she would kill me once I had outlived my usefulness. "Let me guess, you want me to take you to Cherbourg"? "Clever boy", she sneered, "it was intuition that got your girlfriend killed, you think you're so smart don't you, just do what you have to do to get me there under cover of darkness, I'll be watching you like a hawk".

I knew the bearing off by heart having shadowed Poppet on a similar course a few nights before. It was only a slight course change from our current heading and with some minor sail adjustments we were on our way to Cherbourg on starboard tack, heeling over at about twenty three degrees to port, unnecessarily so under normal circumstances, but things were not normal. She was in my world now and I knew I would get my chance to overpower her. Rusty never took his eyes off her either, he seemed to have an aversion to guns and he was keen to pounce, growling if she even moved a finger. "You'd better control that bloody dog unless you want me to put a bullet in him". She would too, so I lay Rusty down and stopped his growling, but he watched her like I did.

She was still standing on the companionway steps with just her head out in the open. I couldn't make her out, on the surface, she came across as a thirty something British woman with no hint of foreign blood or accent, yet she was aggressive and very much involved in terrorism. I tried engaging in conversation with her but in truth, my instinct was to kill her given half a chance. I asked who she was and why she was involved in terrorism against her own country. "None of your business, just concern yourself with getting me to France". When she could see there were no other boats around, she stepped out of the companionway and stood a safe distance away from me with her back leant against the starboard winch in the cockpit.

We were making almost nine knots in a brisk wind and I sensed she was beginning to relax her guard. I'd had to tell Rusty off when she came in the cockpit for fear she might harm him, but he still watched her without blinking. It was her turn to make conversation, "why did the two of you interfere rather than involve the police" she asked, clearly pissed off we had? "You made the mistake of kidnapping our friend and bringing your terrorism to a part of England that still cares for each other". "Didn't work for your Julie did it" she sniped, "and I guess you killed Hannah in cold blood as well", I shot back. She laughed, it was clear that human life meant nothing to her, just her twisted view of violence and the death of innocent human beings. "If I'm not mistaken" I said, " you were born in this country of British parents, so what happened to warp your mind to committing these acts of pure hatred against the country that educated you"? I didn't really want to talk to her, but I needed her to be thinking of something else other than guarding us.

The wind was gusting and just as she was about to answer, I saw my opportunity. "I married a Muslim and he showed me...........". I swung the helm hard over to starboard, we were through the wind in no time and Pilgrim lurched and heeled hard over to starboard as we changed to port tack and the wind caught the sails. She stumbled backwards firing her gun as she went over the cockpit coaming, crashing onto the side rail, dislodging the pistol which slid harmlessly away towards the bow.

I was stepping forward to reach the boat hook on the cabin top when I noticed Rusty had also careered against the starboard side of the cockpit, tumbled over onto the side deck and slid under the guardrail straight into the sea. Hannah was scrabbling to get to her feet, but I had the boat hook in my hand, not an ordinary boat hook like the aluminium ones that float, but a heavy bronzed hook that my Grandfather had made in the machine shop, which now became a lethal weapon and which I brought down on her skull with enough force to kill her. She wasn't finished and neither was I, sparing no mercy, I used it to prod and to beat, she had killed my Julie in cold blood and I would return the favour, an eye for an eye and a tooth for a tooth.

I looked behind the boat, Rusty was OK, he was looking straight at me in the water, trying to swim towards the boat, but we were moving too fast. I had to finish off Hannah before I could rescue him, so I turned my attention back to her, she was bleeding from her head but there was still a snarling fight left in her. She was no match for the boat hook without a weapon of her own, or was it a knife she was trying to retrieve from under her jacket. I didn't care, the beating I was giving her continued, she gave Julie no second chance and neither would she get one from me. I was shouting at her in a rage I didn't recognise, I was turning into an animal no better than her, but neither was I going to make the mistake of showing enough mercy to allow her to come back at me.

I heard a voice in my head calling for me to stop, was this Julie from the afterlife, protecting me from myself? She wasn't given a chance to get back up on her feet, she lay there lifeless, I checked back over my shoulder, Rusty was still there, but much further away by now, bobbing up and down in the swell. I quickly furled all the sails to bring Pilgrim to a halt, opened one of the cockpit lockers and found an old dock line. Still with the boat hook in my hands, I approached Hannah, prodded her some more and when I was satisfied she was out cold, tied both her hands and feet together. I started the diesel and looked over my shoulder for Rusty as I turned the boat around. He was still making his way towards me, typical of Labrador's and Retriever's I thought, they seem so at home in the water. I pulled up alongside him and in no time he was aboard, shaking his coat dry, soaking me in the process. I was so glad he was OK, and his kindly face told me he felt the same way.

I went to the main mast and made a running bowline knot on the end of the main halyard, released the other end off the winch, and went onto the starboard side deck and placed the noose around her scrawny neck. She stirred and those evil eyes met mine. If looks could kill, I would already be dead, but I was in control now. Her instincts were still to attack me, it was just as well that I had secured her hands behind her back and her feet together, otherwise I might have been in trouble.

There are those who would say that what I did next was inhuman, but here was a woman who I knew had killed two people and probably countless others, who had kidnapped and tortured my friend and attempted to kill or maim at least another five hundred innocent people with a powerful bomb. Sadistic I may have become, but my anger was real and seething within my guts. I returned to the winch and started hauling the bitch towards the mast. She was choking, but I knew she would use her feet to push herself to lessen the pressure on her throat. She was slumped at the base of the mast, "stand up" I said, "make me" she retorted, "my pleasure" I said, and started turning the winch handle. She was soon helping, her alternative was to choke to death there and then. For tuppence, I would have hung her from the main mast, but Julie's voice was shouting, imploring me to stop. I hesitated, found another dock line in the locker and trussed her up like a Christmas Turkey to the mast. She spat at me, so I gave the winch handle another turn. Her eyes nearly popped out of her head, but honestly, I didn't care. In the eyes of the law, this was torture, but it was no less than what would have happened to countless people at Langham, who would have lost limbs or their eyesight or even their lives.

  I had no idea I had this ruthless nature within me, but the last few days had sent shock waves through my entire being, and would have finished it there and then if it could have brought Julie back to me. This was not how I had been brought up, tolerance and compassion were inbuilt into our psyche, I took one more look at her face which by now was contorted, I released the winch a few notches and heard a huge intake of breath. I left her there and returned to the cockpit, found the fresh water hose and washed the salt water out of Rusty's coat before drying him off with an old towel. I hauled the foresails and the mizzen and turned the boat back towards Dartmouth.

I hailed Sam on the VHF, "come in Pilgrim, this is Dartmouth Harbourmaster". We changed to channel eight, "is Morgan still with you" I asked"? "Gone home for a bit of shuteye" he said, "get him back to the dock for me would you, I'm on my way back with a toxic cargo he will want to see, should be with you in about forty five minutes". I took out my phone and took a picture of my captive trussed to the mast, not for any gruesome pleasure but as material for Julie's story which I was determined to finish for her.

Hannah tried to persuade me to release her, it was the most talkative she had been since our encounter had begun. "You don't know who I am do you" she said, "if you don't release me, there will be repercussions for you and your family". She was threatening my family now, how I held myself back I don't know but I told her she could be the devil herself and it would make no difference. "They call me the white widow" she claimed, and I know some people who will gladly take your mother's heart out and eat it". I tightened the winch once more which shut her up, but allowed her enough air to survive.

Morgan and Sam were stood on the dock along with several other uniformed and plain clothes officers. They watched me dock Pilgrim and took her lines. They stood speechless at the sight before them. Morgan came on board, "what the hell are you up to Bobby, is she still alive"? "I've kept her alive for you Morgan, just, my instincts were to kill her there and then, which would have been no more than she deserved". I was angry still and Morgan seemed ungrateful that I had done his job for him yet again. "For God's sake, cut her down", there was a crowd gathering on the Quay and Morgan knew that photos would whizz around the world in a matter of seconds through sites like Facebook and twitter. "She was hidden in Pilgrim and threatened me with a gun, she took a fucking shot at Rusty before I managed to overpower the bitch, so don't you bloody preach to me about how I should treat her, she's a bloody terrorist". "Cut her down Bobby, and where's the gun she used"? "It slid down the far side deck" I said pointing over to the starboard side.

Another two officers had come aboard, one helped Morgan and I free her from the mast whilst the other retrieved the gun. "You didn't have to put this noose around her neck Bobby". "You can fuck off Morgan, she's a dangerous terrorist who's killed two people to my knowledge, one of them my Julie, and she would have killed me without hesitation once I'd done what she asked and taken her to Cherbourg. She's bloody lucky I didn't hang her from the main mast".

We cut her down, all the fight had been sucked out of her but she still managed to spit in Morgan's face. "Bitch" he said, and at last he smiled as the officer brought him the gun off the foredeck. I had given her such a beating that she couldn't walk off the boat. Dartmouth hospital was across the road and other officers grabbed a wheelchair and handcuffed her to it. "Do you have any clue as to who she is" he asked. "She claimed to be called the 'white widow' and threatened me and my family with revenge from her 'friends' if I handed her over to you". "Jesus Bobby, if she is who she says she is then you've captured the most wanted woman in the world right now. She's the subject of an Interpol red notice". "We'll you'd better take special care of her then, and get her out of my sight before I regret not ending her miserable life out at sea".

Sam came over and patted me on the back, "what is it with you Bobby, you seem to attract trouble"? "That's the problem, and I've never even gone out of my way looking for it. I hope to God that puts an end to it". Rusty was slowly getting back to his normal self, the tumble off the boat had clearly shocked him and he was still a bit wary as I related the story to Sam, but he wagged his tail each time he heard his name.

Morgan's officers wheeled 'Hannah' over to the hospital for a doctor to give her the once over but before he left, he came over to Sam and I, "sorry I was a bit stroppy with you Bobby, but I've had no sleep for over thirty six hours and I'm a bit cranky. Well done for what you've done, Dartmouth will sleep better tonight, I only wish we could turn the clock back twenty four hours and prevented last night's tragedy". He slapped me on the back and caught up with his men headed towards the hospital. I tidied Pilgrims deck and secured the halyard, my plans had changed again, and I pointed Pilgrim back to Sand Quay.

Chapter 24

Father and Tim were on the dock having just brought back the Blue Dart 120 from the mooring. "You're back early" Tim said, "we didn't expect you back until tomorrow according to the message you left". I told them what had happened and they listened with just the odd "Jesus", and "bloody hell" interrupting me. Father knew exactly who the 'white widow' was, and told us about how her husband had been killed when he set off a suicide bomb on the London Tube. They both questioned how a young woman brought up by a British mother and father, and educated here could turn on her own country, and in such a vicious way. They were even more amazed that she had passed as the housekeeper at Langham for the past three months while they planned this atrocity. "Have you had some lunch Bobby" father asked? The four of us, including Rusty went over to Smugglers Landing and had the longest chat we'd had together forever.

The Regatta 65 was still on her mooring downriver, Tim and I volunteered to fetch her while father organised the cleaning of the motor yacht. Rusty had to come of course, he seemed to have regained his sea legs. She was safely brought back to the dock. It was amazing how much bigger and heavier she seemed than Pilgrim, yet there was only eleven feet difference. I asked Tim it he'd been up to check on 'Beatrice' at Langham's demolished dock. "Went up this morning when I came back from Compton" he said, Police everywhere, they wouldn't let me near her, but from what I could see, she was still afloat, it appears the Lady Elizabeth took the brunt of the blast and 'Beatrice' was shielded. It's a holy mess up there with at least five boats either ruined or sank, and the boathouse will have to be demolished and rebuilt". "You busy" I asked, "let's take another look, they may let us take her away if she's not holed".

I needed to be doing things, as soon as I stopped, Julie would come flooding back into my mind. We took Pilgrim's tender and Rusty was sat bolt upright inside before either one of us climbed aboard. I commented that the 'Magie Noir' had slipped her mooring and disappeared. The French had fled, typical I thought. As we made our way upriver, there was a lot of debris still floating, branches of trees, leaves and bits of boat and as we came closer, the scene became even more depressing with trees stripped of their leaves, branches split but still hanging on. The biggest shock was the dock, or more accurately, the lack of a dock, just splintered pilings sticking out of the water, one of which was stopping the Lady Elizabeth from drifting away. The whole of the port side of the Lady Elizabeth was severely damaged and would need a total refurbishment.

We pulled up close to Beatrice, she didn't seem too badly damaged having been shielded from the worst of the explosion by the bigger boat. She was full of debris, including the red and white roses, which immediately put a lump back in my throat. We were clearing the worst of the rubbish from Beatrice's deck when I noticed one of the windscreens was cracked. We were almost finished when I heard Ricky's voice on the bank, "call the police Grandpa, we've got some looters here already", he laughed, always the comedian. On the bank with him were the Earl, Michael, George and Elizabeth. We joined them on the bank, what a mess the Earl said as he came up to me and embraced me as if I was one of his own. "How are you holding up lad, terrible business, terrible"? "I'm OK Sir" I said. "Hope they catch that Hannah, we treated her as one of the family these three months past and she brings such grief to our little community, especially you young Bobby, after all you did in finding Ricky".

They said the PM was horrified that it had been so easy for these people to enter our country, and she was going to ensure our Border Agency were more vigilant. She had left for her holiday in Cornwall after breakfast, but had asked them to pass her condolences to Julie's family and me. Elizabeth also put her arms around me, she was already crying, I didn't see much of you last night and when Julie died, I just couldn't face anybody. I'm sorry I wasn't there for you Bobby". "Don't worry, she won't harm anyone ever again, the police have her". I thought the men were going to jump in the river for joy, they were so pleased she'd been caught and when I told them how, they were speechless. Ricky was the first to say anything, "if it had been me Bobby, I think I would have hung her there and then too". They all shook their head in agreement, "I hope the courts don't do their usual pitiful job and treat her with any leniency" the Earl said, "I shall have to have a word with some of the Law Lords and fellow peers in the House of Lords".

After putting the world to rights, Tim and I managed to free Beatrice and we had her ready to try the diesel. She amazingly fired up first time and after checking nothing was caught around the prop, Tim reversed her out and checked the rudder. All looked in running order and she manoeuvred forward and back OK. Michael called out that he hoped the yard wasn't too busy as the Lady Elizabeth would need some tender loving care to bring her back to her full glory. I saw a little smile on Tim's face, all work was welcome. We waved our goodbyes and took both the little boats back to their berths.

Morgan was instructed to take Hannah to Police HQ in Exeter as soon as the doctor had given her a check-up. Morgan was not surprised that his superiors were sceptical about Hannah's true identity, especially since she was understood to be in hiding in Kenya. They were still experiencing difficulty in identifying who the kidnapper at Scabbacombe was as the Police National Computer had kicked up no criminal record in the UK. The anti-terrorism squad were liaising with Interpol HQ in Lyon, France, but it was 'le weekend', and progress was slow. Morgan was livid, "terrorists don't take the weekend off" he kept saying, but these cogs only seem to turn at a particular speed, and no amount of pressure seemed to have any effect.

I was restless, everyone told me to take it easy, that I'd suffered a bad shock, but every time I stopped, the bad memories came flooding back. Julie would have wanted me to carry on and she would have especially wanted to write her story, and what a story it turned out to be. It was something I wanted to do for Julie. I had gone out on Pilgrim earlier with every intention of finding a quiet spot to put her story together.

Tim looked up surprised when he heard Pilgrim's diesel fire up again. "Where are you going now Bobby, can't you just sit still"? I told him my plan and he just nodded, "just keep in touch and stay safe" he said. Rusty and I motored down the river and headed towards Torbay.

The wind had eased a little since this morning as we passed the spot where it had all started. Scabbacombe Cottage still had police tape around it, we had been so happy after rescuing Ricky from there, but it had all gone so wrong. Berry Head and the lighthouse came up and although I had decided to head for Torquay Marina, I wanted somewhere more peaceful, so we crossed the bay towards Thatcher Rock and the Ore Stone, before turning towards Babbacombe beach to pick up a mooring at the Cary Arms.

Surrounded by Devon's red sandstone cliffs, which had become increasingly unstable with heavy rain during the winter, the Cary Arms was located in an idyllic position, overlooking Lyme Bay with views all the way over to Portland Bill. The Cary Arms' terraced gardens were busy with people enjoying a drink and some excellent food as the last of the days' sunshine peeped down from Babbacombe Down. I was hungry again and Rusty joined me in a short trip to the jetty where locals and visitors were enjoying some fishing. Rusty was barking, his feet up on the side of the tender, looking down into the water, and there he was, Sammy the Seal, a regular visitor who entertained visitors with his antics. We tied the tender to one of the many rings set into the jetty wall and climbed up through the garden for a well-deserved pint of Devon Red cider and one of their local Brixham crab sandwiches. Rusty of course had to make do with a bowl of water and a few loose biscuits I had popped into my pocket. It was a pleasure to just be alone, no questions, no sympathetic looks or gruff policemen, no nasty terrorist's ready to kill or maim, just me, Rusty and Pilgrim.

We returned to Pilgrim, poured myself another cider and settled down at my laptop to try and do justice to Julie's memory. I had photos, all I had to do was find the right words. My email pinged, mostly junk, but there was one from Ricky, sent an hour earlier with an attached photo. The message read, "You were so happy, made for each other, I wish I could turn back time for you, my true friends". I opened the picture and for the first time found out what the depths of despair really felt like. I cried, a deep anguish gripped my soul, the misery and melancholy of loss, because the picture on the screen was Julie and I dancing together. We looked utterly besotted with each other, Julie looking stunning in her beautiful dress, the diamonds and emerald about her neck, and me, smart in my tuxedo looking at the most beautiful girl in the world. The picture deeply distressed me, but I was so grateful Ricky had taken it, it would be the only memory of the two of us together.

The story wrote itself, written from Julie's point of view, covering the ecstasy and tragedy, goodness and evil, the heroes and villains and the joy and sorrow of the past few days. It was written with a broken heart, with feeling and remorse for getting her involved in something that had snuffed her young life out so violently, when we had both found love. Her father had entrusted me with Julie's obituary, I read it over and over before eventually emailing it to the editors of all the national newspapers and the Dartmouth Breeze.

I poured myself another cider and sat up on deck with Rusty at my side. I could have sworn the old dog had a tear in his eye, as if he knew he would never see her again, but it was probably my illusion, something I wanted to believe was true. The sun had finally dipped below the horizon but the sky continued to glow a deep crimson, promising another glorious summer day. I turned in, exhausted from a day which I thought had brought a nightmare to an end, but fate had another trick up its sleeve.

Chapter 25

The morning of Julie's funeral a week later had dawned with a more autumnal feel to the weather. August had turned into September and with a little chill in the air, the crowds had largely receded and Dartmouth was slowly returning to its more sedate self.

It was a day which I was dreading, for all the memories would flood back along with the gut wrenching sense of loss. The people of Dartmouth were still in a state of shock from a week ago and would turn out in their hundreds to say a last farewell to one of their own. The service at St. Saviours would be at eleven followed by interment at the town's Longcross cemetery, high on the hill overlooking the river.

Father was driving us to St. Saviours with Tim following. Uncle Nathan and his family had gone home with the exception of Amanda who was accompanying Ricky. The Earl and Grandma led us into the church behind Michael and Ellen, George and Elizabeth. Pippa held my arm as I stumbled up the path, which was lined five or six deep with friends and townsfolk who had come to pay their respects. Inside was a sea of people, old and young with the church choir dressed in their red and white either side of the altar. Charlie Fairbrother was already sat closest to Julie's coffin and next to her sister, who I knew had been due to fly in from Florida the day before. They had their backs to me as we sat in the pews behind them, the organist played Elgar's Nimrod from the Enigma Variations.

Father Godfrey welcomed the family and friends of Julie, making no particular reference to the PM, who was sitting near the back of the church with her husband, and had broken their holiday as a mark of respect to Julie, whose action had saved their lives and many more who were at the church.

The service started with the hymn, Abide with Me, of particular significance as it had been written just a few miles away at what was now The Berry Head Hotel, but previously the home of Brixham's vicar, Henry Lyte.

Father Godfrey's prayer of thanks for Julie Fairbrother's life left few of the congregation without tears, me included, yet I had to follow with an eulogy, which choked me up several times. As I had stepped up to the altar and turned, my eyes had descended to where I expected to see Julie's sister Sarah with her Dad, but it was Julie herself who looked back at me. I froze, saying nothing for what must have been an age, as I struggled to compose myself. At that moment, I would have never have believed she had actually died, for Sarah was to me a twin, which unsettled me so much that Father Godfrey's arm around my shoulder was needed to bring me back from a deep shock. As I recited Mary Frye's poem, it was as if it was to Sarah and that somehow the two had become one;

> *"Do not stand at my grave and weep,*
> *I am not there, I do not sleep.*
> *I am a thousand winds that blow.*
> *I am the diamond glint on snow.*
> *I am the sunlight on ripened grain.*
> *I am the gentle autumn rain.*
> *When you wake in the morning hush,*
> *I am the swift, uplifting rush*
> *Of quiet birds in circling flight.*
> *I am the soft starlight at night.*
> *Do not stand at my grave and weep.*
> *I am not there, I do not sleep.*
> *Do not stand at my grave and cry.*
> *I am not there, I did not die!"*

"Julie had agreed to be my wife just before she died. The memories I have are so very short, but the sweetest of my life. May she rest amongst the red and white roses of my love, forever in peace".

As I took my seat, there were no dry eyes in the church that day. The reading from the Book of Ecclesiastes helped heal some deep wounds;

"To everything there is a season, and a time to every purpose under the heaven:

a time to be born, and a time to die;

a time to plant, and a time to pluck up that which is planted;

a time to kill, and a time to heal; a time to break down, and a time to build up;

a time to weep, and a time to laugh; a time to mourn, and a time to dance....."

The service lightened a little as the choir sang "A Time to say Goodbye" before a prayer and the hymn "All things bright and beautiful" rang out with the congregation in full voice.

We stepped out of the church into a murky light which threatened to turn into rain. So many people wanted to share their sympathy with us, it overwhelmed me that the town was so closely knit. I embraced Charlie Fairbrother and all he could say, with tears still in his eyes, was, "you're a good lad Bobby, you made her happy".

I found it so difficult to speak to Sarah, not only did she look like Julie, she even sounded like her, smiled like her, walked like her....... It frightened and stirred me at the same time!

Morgan came over and seemed distant, he was clearly moved and unlike him, lost for words. Pippa and Elizabeth were hugging each other whilst Ricky and Amanda came over and without saying anything, just grabbed me in a show of the closest friendship.

Family and close friends were invited to Longcross Cemetery and a procession of cars followed the hearse up the hill to Julie's final resting place. We waited for the bearers to carry the coffin and followed behind Charlie and Sarah. I had brought Rusty in the car, and he walked by my side to the grave. Charlie smiled weakly on seeing him, but Sarah was overwhelmed and broke down.

A light drizzle was falling and as I looked down onto the river valley, a perfect rainbow spanned the two banks of the Dart, which I took to be a sign of hope in adversity.

It was a very short interment service, I took out the little wooden box that I had saved the red and white rose petals in, and scattered them over Julie's coffin, said my final goodbye, and turned to walk away, but Rusty pulled me back, he was looking down at where she lay, and if I didn't know better, he was saying his own goodbye to Julie.

The wake was at the Royal Castle, ironically where Julie and I had been aware of our earliest attraction. It was a chance for old friends to chat and reminisce and for somehow, life to move on in the knowledge that those who have left us are never forgotten. I gave Charlie back the photos I had borrowed, with a copy of one he didn't have, Julie and I at the Regatta Ball. Sarah couldn't take her eyes off it, it was the most recent picture of Julie, and she was at her most stunningly beautiful. "Can I have a copy too please Bobby" she asked? "Of course you can" I said, "let me have your email address and I'll send you a copy". "When are you flying back to Florida" I asked? "I'm staying a couple of days before I have to be back at work" she said. My heart sank, I'd hoped I might get to know her a little, but I was being insensitive in even thinking it would happen. "You might want to try sailing on the Gulf of Mexico and around Sanibel and Captiva Islands someday" she said, "so keep in touch". My heart missed a beat, is it possible I could fall for Julie's sister? "I've got your details, I'll send you the picture and who knows, I'm sure I'd like that" I said without sounding too forward, but my heart was already pounding in my chest at the thought.

The sun was out again and the river sparkled, the healing had begun.

Chapter 26

The day after the funeral, we were all having a final family breakfast together before I was taking Pippa to the station. She had accepted a new semi-permanent position with the London Symphony Orchestra, and was due back for rehearsals that evening for a forthcoming tour of the Far East. Conversation was subdued, always a sad occasion when the family parted, but it seemed harder today with Julie's funeral the day before and Pippa's relationship with David at an end.

There was a loud rap at the door and father was up, muttering who the hell that was at this early hour. I heard Morgan's voice in the hall, and when I turned the corner, saw he was not alone, there was another uniformed officer who I recognised from the station with him. He looked glum, his demeanour so different to the Morgan I knew, but I remembered that he wasn't himself at the funeral, but put it down to the sad occasion.

"I don't know how to tell you this Bobby, and I sure as hell wasn't expecting to be here to carry it out". "You sound as if someone else has died, what's the matter" I asked. He took a paper from his inside pocket, I have a warrant for your arrest here Bobby, and I'm afraid you're going to have to come with me to Exeter". Father and I were speechless, but it was father who spoke first, "an arrest warrant", he asked incredulously, "on what charge for God's sake"? "Two counts of Grievous Bodily Harm and one of Attempted Murder" he said, not believing it himself. I was still dumb with shock, "and who's made these ridiculous charges" he asked? Morgan looked at me, "Ricky's kidnapper at Scabbacombe and the bitch you tied to your mast with a noose around her neck, and what makes matters worse, she's got proof, pictures that were taken by members of the public when you pulled up at the dock were posted on 'YouTube' went viral in minutes, so we have no choice but to follow it up".

A heated argument ensued in the hall with mother and father shouting at Morgan and Tim and Pippa throwing in their pennyworth. "Don't shoot the messenger" Morgan said, "the warrants were issued yesterday and I was instructed to carry out the arrest immediately. I had to threaten to resign unless they allowed twenty four hours grace for you to attend Julie's funeral, but I'm sorry Bobby, I have to take you in now".

Morgan read my rights and the hall fell silent as we all looked from one to another. "Can I assume that I will not be coming home tonight, so do I need to pack my toothbrush"? I had found my voice again and I was being sarcastic, but anger was rising which I was struggling to control, but I also knew it would only make matters worse if I resisted. At least it explained why Morgan was cold towards me at the funeral. Five minutes later, I was on my way to Exeter in the back of Morgan's police car and Pippa was on her way to Totnes with Tim.

Father was on the phone to our lawyer's, a firm in Exeter who promised to be at the police station within half an hour. We drove mostly in silence, Morgan trying his best to reassure me that it would be thrown out before going to court. My mind was running amok, was this really happening or was it some sick joke? Why would they charge me when the criminals had kidnapped and murdered already, and had tried to murder or maim another five hundred people? It made no sense, it had to be a mistake, but I felt very insecure at that moment.

We arrived at the Exeter Police HQ, which ironically was where the three terrorists had also been held, I was shown to the desk, booked in and held in a custody cell. I heard Morgan tell the duty sergeant to look after me, and I also thought I heard him say it was a travesty of justice that I was there at all. I sat alone in the cell, almost in a trance, it was as if my brain couldn't comprehend what was happening to me.

They did bring me some tea and biscuits but it was a whole hour before two officers took me into an interview room. I had a very basic knowledge of my rights and they ensured that I understood why I was there. They duly informed me that I had not been charged with the offences yet, and that I was merely helping them to determine whether there was a case to answer. They were just about to start their questioning when an uniformed officer came in, my lawyer, a Mr Andrew Jones had just arrived and they left the two of us alone to get acquainted.

Eventually, the interrogation got underway, and once the preliminaries had been completed, a photo of the man at the cottage was shown to us, except that it was taken at the hospital where he had received treatment for a broken leg, fractured shoulder and some bruising. "Did you cause this man's injuries" was the question they asked. I looked at my lawyer who indicated that I should not answer the question. "No comment" I said. A second photo was placed on the table, of the man at the Regatta Ball from who I had received, rather than given a beating to, but with some superficial bruising on his face and body. Again my lawyer shook his head, same answer. Finally, a rather graphic picture of the 'white widow', tethered to Pilgrim's mast and with the halyard looped around her neck was placed on the table, and the question and answer was the same, "no comment".

I was confused as each of those photos could easily be construed as 'self-defence', but my lawyer clearly was not prepared at this stage to either confirm, deny or defend anything, he wanted to see what evidence the police had before having time to consider our defence. The officers were clearly frustrated and suggested I seriously considered the consequences of not co-operating. Copies of the photos were provided along with the arrest warrants and we were left alone to discuss each of the allegations. After more than an hour we had concluded that the GBH charges were easily defended but the most damning evidence were the pictures on the boat. Mr Jones did not want to disclose any probable defence at this stage, and we agreed to wait and see whether the police would formally charge me. They also chose to play cagily and remanded me in custody pending further investigations. It was a cat and mouse game which neither Mr Jones nor I could fathom why it was being pursued in view of the allegations having been made by terrorists.

I was taken back to my cell to sweat it out, and other than food brought in by the duty officer. I was in jail for the first time in my entire life and I was frightened, although I had not been charged with anything, yet, but they had twenty four hours, which meant I was going to be locked up for the night.

Father was fuming, neither Tim nor mother had ever seen him in such a rage, all targeted at the stupid Criminal Justice system, which better served the criminal rather than looking after the victims of crime. "Bloody left wing do-gooder's" he kept shouting, at nobody in particular. He had been advised by Mr Jones that I would likely be charged in the morning but would be released on police bail pending a hearing at the Magistrates Court to determine whether there was a case to answer. It was unusual that a person charged with Attempted Murder would get bail, but the circumstances surrounding these allegations were "stacked in our favour".

My father came to collect me in the morning, I had as expected been charged and released to his custody, and a date for the Magistrates hearing was set in one week. We arrived home in time for lunch which I devoured as if it had been the last meal of a condemned man!

That week was frantic, telephone calls, meetings with our barrister and most importantly, gathering whatever evidence we could muster to defend the charges. Unbeknown to me, there had also been some heavy top end political pressure with The Earl, Sir Michael and Ted, the Hon. Edward Gilbert MP, including the Lady Beatrice my Grandmother and father, Sir Robert Hawley.

The Crown Prosecution Service were already under some intense pressure following a series of 'celebrity witch hunts' which had failed to deliver any guilty verdicts, and questions were being asked about the police and CPS's competence in pursuing cases against the victims of crime who were defending family, friends or their property.

More important to me was that the people of Dartmouth had begun a petition calling for the charges to be dropped in view of the countless lives that had been saved by Julie and my actions. The petition had already collected five thousand signatures locally and was going ballistic when a Facebook campaign had been started. Ricky was in on the act, drumming up support on line and for me personally.

Two days before the hearing, my father took a call from a local freelance photographer who asked if he could meet with us. Kevin Miller came up to Hawley that evening and father and I sat with him in the study. "I'm sorry I haven't contacted you sooner" he said, "but what I have here is both incriminating and very upsetting at the same time. I never go anywhere without my camera, which upsets people rather a lot. You may think that the pictures I took at the Regatta Ball are inappropriate, and I would admit that some are, but I also have some that may help you Bobby, but I warn you, they are also distasteful".

Father and I thought he was a bit of a weirdo, and we looked at each with raised eyebrows several times. However, when he started placing the photos on father's desk, we realised this man might turn out to be our saviour. The pictures started off fairly mildly with a man rolling a barrel towards the marquee. As the scene developed, a frame caught him kneeling by the barrel and a red light clearly visible. The next sequence showed me approaching and my challenge, which resulted in a severe beating, but the barrel is seen crashing off a trestle with me falling to the ground. Importantly, there's also a picture of two men pinning my assailant to the ground. This chap may have been a bit strange, but it was clear to both of us that he knew what he was doing with a camera.

"Mr Hawley, these next photos will upset you so please be prepared". I was already tense, having seen the detail of the previous photos, I was bracing myself, thinking that I knew what to expect. I was so wrong, what confronted the two of us made us think this man was sick, for it captured Julie's murder in the most gruesome and graphic detail, especially shots taken at close range, even the moment the knife had plunged into her chest and the bloody aftermath. I retched, I felt violently sick and had to hurry out of the room before embarrassing myself.

When I returned, father had already seen the pictures of me cradling a dying Julie, even the diamond and emerald ring being placed on her finger. Recovering from the trauma of re-living the most traumatic moment of my life, I realised that although I now hated this man, this peeping Tom who used his camera to prey on people's private lives, in this instance, he had captured crucial evidence. Julie's killer was photographed in full colour, both committing the murder and later pressing the buttons which exploded the bomb. The photos also showed why the police failed to capture her in the immediate aftermath, as Kevin had recovered to take pictures of people scrambling for cover or lying on the floor, except for 'Hannah Parker' who was disappearing into Langham Wood amongst the flying debris and mayhem.

I couldn't look at the pictures of Julie, her dress covered in blood, but father later told me they were indeed distasteful beyond belief. Kevin Miller was by now very wary of the hurt he was causing and of my increasing horror at his insensitivity. "I don't know whether the pictures I took down at the Quay the following day will be of help to you, but there are three which may be of interest". The first almost identical to the photo the police presented to me in Exeter, showing her strapped to the mast with the noose around her neck whilst I stood on the boat with a docking line in my hand. The second graphically caught poor Morgan within range of a cloud of spit heading his way out of Hannah's mouth, and the third of an uniformed officer just after he had retrieved the gun she had threatened me with and fired.

There were others, including Hannah in a wheelchair, but were certainly of no use to us from a defence standpoint. The feeling cursing through my veins was one of disgust coupled with gratitude, I didn't like him but neither did I hate him, because these photos proved that Hannah was very much alive and kicking and spitting when I brought her back to the dock that day. She certainly showed no signs that she had been beaten to within an inch of her life, nor that there had been an attempt to murder her.

Father took a cheque book from his desk drawer and asked Kevin how much we owed him. In fairness, he declined any money but my father insisted, requesting him send us the digital files which he agreed he would, and was more than delighted with the five hundred pounds father paid him.

After Kevin left, we both agreed that he was a dangerous little man, but very useful. "Whilst we're on the subject of photos" father said, "Sir Michael sent us these in case they were helpful". They were the ransom demands from Ricky's kidnappers with the pictures of him following the beatings he had received. We were scheduled for a final meeting with our Barrister the following day and father and I merged the photos, including ones of my gunshot wound which fortunately had been taken at Morgan's request at the hospital. "Thank the Lord for digital cameras and phones" I said, as I went for a walk to clear my head. Rusty didn't leave my side these days, it was almost as if he thought that by sticking with me, I would lead him to Julie.

We walked down Hawley's long gravel drive towards Long Wood and the marina. I hadn't been near Pilgrim since returning from Babbacombe almost a week before, a week I wasn't going to forget for a while, but wished I could. As we passed under the railway bridge, the steam train clanked and whistled overhead. The marina had quietened down with many of the berths now empty, but Pilgrim stood proud in the hazy sun, she needed a good clean in and out so the two of us rolled up our sleeves, or in Rusty's case, made the job twice as difficult as it need have been, constantly biting my deck brush and threatening to knock over the bucket of soapy water. The hull had a few stains from the fenders which quickly came off, but she would need a good polish before winter set in. "Now for the inside Rusty" I said, "where you'll be even less help than you were on the outside".

I cleared and polished the saloon, then the master stateroom. Somehow, Julie was still in there, watching me, smiling, mocking my feeble attempt at housework. I smiled back, "I'm a mere man" I said out loud, not sure who to. Next, the forward berth in the V-deck, I stopped, remembering that it was here that the gun was thrust in my face. I hadn't been in there since but it shocked me that it was so untidy, the head door was wide open and the bed was covered in food she had clearly taken from the fridge.

Rusty was barking again, picking up the scent of an undesirable no doubt. I walked in, black bin liner in hand, but went flying, tripping on something in the gloom of the cabin whose blinds were down. I landed prostate on the bed amongst the remnants of scraps of dinner and behind me, on the floor was a rucksack which did not belong on Pilgrim.

I took it out into the light of the saloon and carefully opened the small outer flap. Inside, I could see a mobile phone, a notebook and two pens, a folded sheet of paper which looked like a hand drawn map with two or three SIM cards loose in the bottom. The main compartment was zipped and upon opening it, I stiffened and very slowly put the rucksack down on the saloon table. Inside was what looked like a suicide belt, which I had only ever seen on films, but here I was, sharing my beautiful boat with one. My initial reaction was to call Morgan, but I hesitated, having completely lost faith in the police, although I felt Morgan was still on my side. I suddenly shuddered with fear, what if moving it had triggered some sort of timer, I had to take another look. I lifted the flap gently, and just as I looked inside, there was a loud rap, rap, rap which made me jump half out of my skin. "You in there Bobby"? It was Dave Parsons, the bugger seemed to have the knack of turning up and winding me up far too often. "Don't come aboard Dave, I've just found another bloody bomb". "What is it with you Bobby, you seem to attract trouble like most people collect debts, are you sure it's a bomb"? I had opened the flap again, "definitely explosives, what looks like a detonator with wires leading to a small pack with a battery and a display like a smart phone".

I closed the flap and carefully helped Rusty up the companionway steps, followed and was stood next to Dave in a flash. "You'd better clear this area Dave" I said, and off he went like a scolded cat. I called Morgan first, "leave the bomb squad to me" he said, "and get everyone out of there, you included Bobby, that's an order, for God's sake, leave it to the police this time". I couldn't resist the snipe, "my confidence in the competence of the police is not exactly very high at the moment Morgan, but this one I will leave with you". I climbed back on-board Pilgrim, "stay Rusty," I called. Dave was screaming at me from the Quay, "Bobby, for Christ's sake what are you playing at, get off that fucking boat". "Won't be a second Dave" as I returned to the saloon. There may be something in that notebook or on the map or even on the phone and SIM cards that may be either useful, or could be used as a bargaining chip in my defence, but I didn't trust the police any more to help me. I checked every nook and cranny of that rucksack and took everything except the bomb, put them in my crew bag which was on-board along with my laptop and climbed back onto the dock.

"You're bloody stupid Bobby, what can be more important than your life"? He had a point of course, but I was on a mission to finish the job Julie and I had started.

Morgan and another officer came running down the Quay towards Smugglers Landing where Dave and I, along with a dozen or so others had retreated for a pint. He was out of breath, panting like an old steam engine, "careful Morgan, at this rate we'll need an ambulance as well as the bomb squad". "There's one on its way you cheeky bugger, along with a fire engine for your information! Now tell me, what are we faced with on the boat"? I filled him in, watched him put some tape at a safe distance to keep people away and we waited. Who arrived next, complete with camera was Kevin Miller, I wasn't surprised, he must monitor all the emergency services frequencies I thought. Morgan was back, satisfied that everyone was safe, "so what's the form when the bomb squad arrives then" I asked? "Normally they send in a remote controlled robot, but they won't be able to on the boat, so I expect one of them will get suited and booted and go and take a look". "So when they've established that it really is a bomb, what do they do then" I asked? "If it can be made safe without risk, they will, otherwise it will have to be a controlled explosion" he said.

My mind stated racing, a controlled explosion on Pilgrim would destroy her. Never in a million years would I contemplate that. Dave looked at me as if he knew what was going through my mind. He shook his head, "don't you even think about it Bobby". Morgan was faffing around like an old hen again because a car had parked too close and the occupants, an elderly couple out to lunch were being nosey. "Keep Rusty here" I said to Dave, and whilst Morgan was fussing over the couple, I hurried down the dock and before Morgan had missed me, I was on-board lowering the tender into the water. He heard the sound of the pulleys, looked up and I think I saw all the veins pop up on his forehead, he certainly changed colour to a bright scarlet as he shouted some profanities my way.

My course of action was already clear and no interference would derail me, other than getting blown up of course. I decided to use the oars as I wasn't going far, the rucksack was gingerly placed on the floor of the tender and I rowed a little way out into the river, headed just around the corner into Noss Creek where there were no people, cars, and more importantly to me, no Pilgrim to be destroyed in a controlled explosion! Morgan was still frantically waving and shouting at me from the dock, I heard amongst other expletives, "you fucking idiot", but ignored him. The whole exercise took ten minutes, I pulled the tender onto the creek's Northern bank where only a few trees and possibly the railway line would be affected by a blast.

I walked back around the creek's cove to the marina as if I'd been out on a Sunday afternoon stroll, and was just about to be attacked by a very angry Morgan when to my relief, two vehicles belonging to the bomb squad arrived. "The package is in the bottom of the boat" I said nonchalantly, pointing to where I'd left it and walked back towards Dave to finish my pint. "You're unbelievably stupid at times you know Bobby, especially for a highly educated rich kid I mean, who just happens to be my employer's son", he laughed! "Maybe I am" I said, "and maybe it was my actions that got Julie killed, or possibly killed by a bomb along with a whole load more people if we had done nothing, but the police, Jesus, if we wait for them to do anything, they chase after the people who's trying to help them. I'm looking after myself from now on Dave".

We watched them take an hour getting their little tracked robot out to the boat, use its mechanical claws to open the rucksack's flap and study the images transmitted back from its camera. Eventually, a heavily suited man walked over and within a few minutes had removed it from the rucksack and made it safe. It was indeed a suicide vest or small waistcoat which according to Morgan could have either been detonated remotely or by the wearer.

I received my customary warning from Morgan, nodded and agreed I was a foolish little boy and went and retrieved my 'little boy's toy', as Morgan had called it, and took it back to Pilgrim. The whole time I was being lectured, Dave stood behind Morgan sniggering and trying to get me into even more trouble. "You call me childish" I said after Morgan had gone, "you're bloody worse than I am"!

Back on Pilgrim, I took out the notebook and the crude map, there were initials and what looked like mobile phone numbers, pages of notes in what looked like Arabic, hand drawings which made no sense to me along with scribbling's that I could not decipher. The map too was hand drawn, but there was a familiarity to it, a long wide street with a small square in the middle and a side street with what looked like a gated entrance all leading to a roundabout. On the map were crosses and asterix with notes in the margins which were either in a foreign language or coded. None of it made sense, I decided not to switch on the mobile phone, put everything back in my crew bag and finished cleaning the forward berth and head.

Father was aghast when I told him what had happened that afternoon and I was told off again for being a "silly little boy" which was starting to wear thin especially since I was all of twenty seven years old! I showed him the documents and the phone, he couldn't make sense of them either but we agreed that they could be a bargaining chip for my Hearing at Exeter Magistrates Court. Something good might come out of it.

Chapter 27

The day before the hearing, father and I met with our lawyer Andrew Jones and our barrister, a Mr Stephen Sheppard at his chambers on St. David's Hill in Exeter. He was an astute man, a little pompous but very sure of himself. He had reviewed the case notes and the evidence that was available from the police. He dismissed the GBH charges saying he would get them dropped at tomorrow's hearing. It was the attempted murder charge which concerned him. He was a little dismissive at first when we spoke of the photos we had but warmed up considerably as we weighed through them. The images of Julie continued to haunt me but we pressed on.

He began to conjure a way of manipulating a capitulation by the CPS as soon as we told him of the suicide bomb found on Pilgrim the day before, which had without question been left there by this "white widow". We showed him the other documentation and the phone, he was initially concerned that we had not handed them over to the police, but followed up by suggesting "that you subsequently found them hidden on the boat when cleaning".

As a result of the 'new evidence', he excused himself and went to make a call to the Detective Inspector leading the case. He was in a confident mood when he returned, "I have arranged a pre-hearing meeting with all parties at nine o'clock tomorrow morning" he said, "and I am confident we can get the case dismissed". "Mr Hawley", he was referring to me, "do you think you can keep yourself out of trouble until tomorrow morning" he asked sarcastically? "I'll do my very best Sir", I replied.

The signatories to the petition had continued to grow with one of the major national newspapers championing the campaign. We were also unaware of the mounting political pressure behind the scenes. Ricky was organising a demonstration outside the Magistrates Court in the morning but a call later in the afternoon from a concerned Andrew Jones wanted it stopped. "We believe we have the police cornered" he said, "so we don't think it's a good idea to embarrass them further". A call to Ricky confirmed that three coaches were destined for Exeter in the morning, and countless more people would turn up as a result of the Facebook campaign, but he agreed to stop whatever he could, "but I can't guarantee that nobody will turn up, you know what students are like" he said.

The whole family had wanted to travel to Exeter with me in the morning, and although we had tried to explain that the case may be dismissed, "we can always go and do a bit of shopping" mother and Grandma had said. Father seemed confident but I was still apprehensive of the outcome.

There was a small gathering with placards outside the court building but we went in unnoticed. We were shown into one of the court's side offices, relationships seemed strained, the police and crown prosecutors one side and myself with just Andrew Jones and Stephen Sheppard QC either side. My Barrister quickly took charge in his confident manner, and whilst he received resistance to start with, this soon melted away when he presented the new evidence and supporting photos. "Gentlemen" he continued, following yesterday's incident on the boat, Mr Hawley recovered additional evidence which we believe will ensure the successful conviction of the people you have in custody, but further, and more importantly may prevent another attack and possibly lead you to others in their organisation". They were all ears and almost begging to do a deal there and then, and when he showed them the contents of the notebook and the phone and map, I guessed we were home and dry and began to relax a little.

He had presented me as a "good citizen" rather than a criminal who had tried to murder anyone and portrayed me as a victim and not a perpetrator. He was brilliant, smooth, precise, almost silky, he had them eating out of his hand. I was mesmerised myself and I thought then that they had come into the meeting knowing they would be eaten alive for lack of solid evidence, they were beaten men, and capitulated.

The hearing which followed was a formality, all charges were dropped and I was a free man.

Epilogue

How different Dartmouth is when the summer visitors have migrated north and East. The creeks, streams and rivers continue their flow to the sea from the high moor, but boat traffic is reduced to the regular ferries and the occasional pleasure craft, although the sailing club continued to hold events well after Regatta Week had finished.

After years of animosity, the houses of Langham and Hawley had grown close, especially with the forthcoming marriage of The Earl to my Grandmother, the Lady Beatrice in the spring. Tim too had found true love, he and the Lady Georgina were engaged, with a summer wedding to look forward to. Elizabeth had broken her engagement and was still working at Imperial College in London. Ricky and I were best buddies, but any notion that he might mend his ways after his abduction at the hands of a beautiful woman were ill-founded and his tendency to drink to excess and womanise remained intact, but he was fun to be with and in many ways I envied his fun loving spirit.

Julie was never far from my thoughts, but father had kept me occupied at the yard which was exceptionally busy with repairs following the blast and an overwhelmingly successful boat show at Southampton which had resulted in a strong order book, including one from The PM's husband Tom Williams for a customised Regatta 65 to be delivered to The Bahamas in time for their Spring break.

Morgan too was back to his ebullient self having been promoted to Detective Inspector. He had collared me in The Royal Castle one evening with the news that the notebook and map had led to the arrest of several suspected terrorists operating in London, and had likely prevented an incident planned for the Armistice parade at The Cenotaph in Whitehall. Guilty verdicts at The Old Bailey had condemned the three that had brought such anguish to Dartmouth to life imprisonment, with a minimum of thirty five years each to the men and forty five years to the 'white widow'. Nina too was rotting in a French prison, she was already on the wanted list for an attempted bombing at Strasbourg Cathedral some years before. Hanging for terrorists and certain other crimes were debated again in Westminster with the inevitable rejection despite public opinion.

Julie had been posthumously awarded The George Cross, the second highest commendation, for her bravery in saving the lives of countless people, along with an OBE for myself in the New Year's

Honours list which Ricky, or more likely, his Uncle Ted, The Foreign and Commonwealth Minister and local Member of Parliament had recommended. I had accompanied Julie's father, a very proud Charlie Fairbrother to Buckingham Palace to receive the honours from the Queen. We had both visited Julie's grave at Longcross with the medals on our return, a very emotional moment.

Julie's sister, Sarah, had returned to Florida before I had a chance to give her the photos of Julie, but we had been in touch through Facebook and occasionally Skype. Every time I saw her face it unnerved me, she was Julie's double which almost made me feel as if she'd never gone away. We had promised to keep in touch, and it was more than likely we would meet up in the spring when I delivered the boat to The Bahamas. I couldn't wait!

Rusty and I enjoyed every moment we could on The Dart, the most beautiful river in the world, which flowed through our beloved Dartmouth. This is Pilgrim's River.

About the Author

Wyn Hughes was born and raised in North Wales before attending Emanuel School in London. Following seven years with British Telecom, he joined Intel in Wiltshire where he lived for twenty years. He has two children and two step children. Wyn moved to Florida with his wife Jan to operate their boat charter business, extensively sailing in the Gulf of Mexico and the Florida Keys. Returning to Britain, they now live in Torquay on the English Riviera, and continue to sail England's South Coast. Pilgrim's River is his first novel and he is already writing the sequel

Made in the USA
Charleston, SC
26 June 2014